# DRAGON AVENGED

## IMMORTAL DRAGONS EPILOGUE

OPHELIA BELL

# CHAPTER 1

*A* warm spring breeze roused Numa from an afternoon post-coital doze. She hummed softly under Zephyrus's caress and shifted positions only to realize that the West Wind was no longer lying beside her in bed. The breeze tugged at her tangled hair, flowed down her shoulders, and lifted the silken sheet, tossing it off before nudging her into full alertness.

"Zeph?" She frowned, darting a look around the lush quarters in the Haven's palace that she and her mates had called their own for the past year. She'd made love to Zephyrus and Dionysus earlier that afternoon, opting for a recharge and a nap while her other three mates joined the crew of nymphs preparing for the Equinox festivities just two days away.

The wind swirled around her and she puffed out an irritated cloud of green smoke. Zeph's magic caught it and shaped the cloud into an arrow aimed at the doorway to the room.

"Fine, I'm coming," she muttered, slipping out of the bed and summoning a gown to drape over her as she headed into the corridor. She followed the little ball of green smoke as the breeze toyed with it, pushing it in a haphazard spiral ahead of her.

The palace was a maze of crystalline corridors that gave the illusion of being underwater, with blue light filtering through in eerie ripples. She missed her home in the Glade with its wide open skies, multitudes of high clifftops, and plenty of room to stretch her wings, but the Haven was the better place for Dion to rest while they waited for his powers to regenerate.

Her body still hummed with the remnants of their last coupling, a sure sign that he was nearly at full divine power again. She followed the breeze through a pair of double doors out onto a palatial covered porch where she paused and took him in, the extent of his recovery hitting her for the first time since he'd lost his powers.

He was leaning against a column, gazing down onto the activities below. His huge, muscular body was relaxed and languid, the same light breeze toying with his silken black curls. Zephyrus leaned on the balustrade across from him, lean and silver-haired, the worry lines beside his mouth completely gone as he regarded the god with affection. Laughter drifted up from the courtyard, along with her other mates' voices raised in amused banter. Zephyrus saw her first, his eyes lighting up before darting a meaningful glance at Dionysus.

Her beautiful god practically glowed with health and vigor, and the marked difference in his size was even more apparent now that he was standing next to Zephyrus, rather than lying on his back while she rode his cock to oblivion. He was healed.

Dion said something she couldn't hear over the noises from the courtyard. He glanced at Zeph, then followed the West Wind's gaze to Numa. His lips tilted in a cocky smile and he turned around to face her fully, leaning back against a column.

"You're awake," he said. "I worried I gave you too much at the end. Did I finally find your limit, little one?"

"Impossible. You know better." Her chest warmed and she couldn't resist smiling at his taunt.

"Indeed," he rumbled, his burgundy gaze sliding down her body like a caress, promising that he lived for nothing more than to keep testing her limits.

Numa sauntered toward him, returning the look with a brazen one of her own, but taking the time to thoroughly inspect his aura while she closed the distance. The magic surrounded him in a brilliant golden glow, stronger than she'd seen it in ages, but that wasn't the only signal of his returning strength. He was a full head taller than Zeph, not counting the pair of thick horns that protruded from his head high enough to graze the ceiling. A year earlier he'd barely been taller than Numa, after his power had been sapped in his effort to control their enemy long enough for them to vanquish the evil bitch. Six months ago he'd finally surpassed Cade's size again and was gradually growing, though his horns were only nubs. She'd been aware of the changes, subtle though they were, but until now it hadn't really registered how close he was to his true divine self again.

"Welcome back," she said. "Just in time for the celebration."

She slipped up to the balustrade between Dion and Zeph, her entire being warming at their proximity. Below them, the main courtyard of the palace was alive with activity. Nymphs darted around, draping flowered garlands over everything. Theron and Bekim were at one end with Cade, adding the final pieces to the roof of a pavilion that the nymphs were already swarming over to decorate.

Her three ursa mates hopped down a few moments later and stood back to admire their handiwork. Numa could barely see the artistry due to the throng of nymphs adding the finishing touches. Finally the activity slowed, and they all paused and oohed and ahhed over the finished spectacle.

"What is it for?" she asked.

"Spring fertility rites," Dion said, then bent close and rumbled, "and none too soon." He dropped one big hand to her ass and squeezed. "Now that I'm at full strength, we can put that baby into you that you wished for."

As if attuned to Dion's voice, the three ursa turned and looked up at them. Numa's breath quickened at the expectant looks in their eyes. The baby she wished for had been just a dream for the past year. With five mates, it had been impossible for her to choose which should have the honor of impregnating her, and so she'd resisted allowing it to happen accidentally. Dion had finally urged her to confess her true wish—and so she'd admitted her desire to somehow have a child made from all of them, which she knew was a ridiculous thing to hope for, if not impossible.

"Oh . . . can we really?" she asked, darting a hopeful look up at Dion, then to Zephyrus, and finally down to Cade, Bekim, and Theron below, who looked like they were ready to leap the two-story distance to reach her and take care of business on the spot.

Zephyrus lightly stroked her cheek. "With Dion's power, we can."

"But not today," Dion said.

"Oh," Numa said, deflating.

Dion's laughter boomed through the courtyard, infecting everyone below with mirth. Nymphs dove into the fountain and splashed each other playfully, their games swiftly turning to carnal fun.

"Soon, little one," he said, sliding his hand up her back.

"My power has returned, it's true, but there is far more to be had in two days on the Equinox." He turned and tucked a fingertip under her chin, urging her to look up at him. "There is a more dire concern to address first."

The one worry they had all been acutely aware of, yet avoided discussing most days would finally need to be addressed. "The bloodline," Numa said.

Dion nodded down toward the orgy of nymphs that were now tangled half in and half out of the fountain. A pair of the recently returned Thiasoi satyrs dove into the fray to the delighted squeals of the females. "They are already feeling my return to power, but my link to the nymphaea is nothing new. Meri's bloodline is mine now too, and the humans who are part of it may be a danger to the higher races once it fully affects them."

Zephyrus twisted his mouth in amusement at the scene unfolding below. Cade had a pair of nymphs clinging to him, very patiently attempting to peel the two females off on his way into the palace. "No doubt it won't be nearly as fun for the humans as it is for them. My brothers have been monitoring things in the human world. They have begun to see signs of awareness in the humans with the bloodline, but since we warned all the higher races to go to ground before the Equinox, these humans are only noticing each other. They don't understand what it means yet."

Apprehension twisted in Numa's gut and she clenched her teeth. She forced herself to relax when her three ursa mates entered and joined the conversation. "We can't expect all our kind to hide for fear of discovery. The dragons have done enough hiding."

"We're all tired of pretending," Cade said, crossing his arms. "The Ultiori have been dismantled. How much danger are we really in if the humans of the bloodline discover the truth?"

"There are millions scattered around the globe with the potential to recognize any of the higher races for who we are," Dion said. "How they react remains to be seen, but the larger concern is allowing that knowledge to become widespread. If modern human communication is as powerful as I understand it is, without intervention of some sort, all of humanity might know of our existence within a matter of days. It would be dangerous for it to happen that quickly. We need to control the flow of information, and that begins with the bloodline."

Numa gazed up at Dion, curious. "You already have a plan, don't you? Do you have enough power to control the entire bloodline?"

Dion smiled bitterly. "Potentially, but that would be the wrong approach. Meri's methods of mind control are not what I wish to employ to handle this challenge. There is the added complication of the mutations many of the humans possess. The bloodline is as varied as Deva's, though none of the humans with it possess more than a few drops of divine power, thanks to their link to me. And they all have souls. Attempting to meddle with them unwillingly could corrupt them."

Numa pursed her lips, following the thread of Dion's thoughts. Meri's creation of the Ultiori had involved infusing humans with the blood of the higher races, her own in particular. Once her puppets interbred, that blood, along with Meri's nymphaea blood, was passed down the generations for thousands of years, their numbers increasing to the millions. It had allowed Meri access to immense power at the end, a power that had nearly cost them control of the Source. If Dionysus hadn't intervened, Meri could have beaten them. Now their biggest worry was being discovered by all of humanity, which had its own set of complicated drawbacks. They couldn't treat this issue lightly.

"But you have the power to reach them, right?" she asked.

"Yes. I can sense all the souls attached to the bloodline, but I can't affect them on my own. I would need power from all five races to do that, and a conduit through which to channel the power—someone with a link to all the races too."

"Not a fucking chance."

Numa's gaze shot to Cade, who had spoken. The big blond ursa shook his head and scowled.

"Cade, you don't even know who would possess that kind of link."

"The hell I don't. You know as well as I do it's Deva he's talking about. The poor girl's been through enough the past year, being shuttled around like precious cargo between all the higher realms, never once allowed to get her feet under her. Now you want her to be the apex of some sex ritual. She isn't ready."

"He never said . . ." Numa objected, but Cade interrupted her with a laugh.

"Sweet pea, you think I don't know how this works? Anything that involves our magic—especially dragon or nymphaea magic—requires someone getting fucked. If it were any one of us, I'd be all over it. The five of us together brought enough power to win a fucking war. But we've got experience under our belts. Eons of it between us. Deva may look old enough—she may be wise beyond her years after living with the gods while we won that war—but she's still a baby, and I guarantee none of her parents are going to sign on, either. Find someone else."

She turned a worried gaze to Dion. "He's right. There has to be someone else who can do it. Meri experimented on thousands. We should at least talk to Neph and Nyx about it, don't you think?"

"You forget I am linked to all the potential options, little one. If they were tainted by Meri's blood, they are now part of *my* bloodline. That includes your brother, who was Meri's first. Yes, I can sense him with Neph and Vrishti and their new daughter in the Sanctuary, though his blood meld to my son is a stronger link. I agree we should open up the conversation to the others when they arrive, but if there was any other option, I would know."

Not prepared to give up the argument, Numa racked her brain for other options. Deva's parents—at least her biological parents, Neela and Nikhil—were the only options that made sense, but Dion would have the final say whether either of them possessed the needed combination of blood.

She accompanied Dion and her other four mates down to the grand hall where Nyx and Nereus were preparing to greet the first wave of guests arriving for the celebration, yet could come up with no other ideas.

The saving grace was that Deva was in the Dragon Glade spending time with her mother, so they would have time yet to discuss the options before she arrived. Neela and her mates had chosen the Glade as their permanent residence owing to Neela's phoenix nature, and Deva spent a few weeks at a time there, learning to harness her own dragon powers under the instruction of her half-sister, Asha. She was a quick study, though the power she exhibited was weak compared to other members of each race.

Numa had received regular messages from Deva over the past year, including the occasional visit, and had never sensed any dissatisfaction in the girl's situation or a struggle to adapt. On the contrary, despite having no soul, Deva's aura carried a patina of hard-earned wisdom belying her true age and she took to her lessons easily. If Numa hadn't been there the day she was born, she'd have believed Deva was as ancient as any of the dragons.

They arrived at the entrance to the grand hall in time to see three figures appear just outside in a cloud of dense fog.

When the mist cleared, Numa rushed forward with an exclamation of delight. "Aodh! Brother, you're here!" She embraced him, then Vrishti and Neph in turn, and stood back beaming at them. "Where is the little one? Is she as much of a joy as she was when I last saw her?"

Vrishti's face split into a glowing smile. "She is the loveliest baby, but the kinds of celebrations going on here during the Equinox aren't exactly appropriate for little ones." She shot a coy look at her mates.

Neph chuckled. "As much as we adore her, we are more than ready for a vacation. Sathmika and the other ursa elders have opened up the Rainsong Lodge for anyone who is in similar straits and wants a respite from their offspring. I've lost count of how many babies have been born over the past year. If we aren't careful, they'll have the run of the Sanctuary by the time we return."

"With hope, we will be adding our own soon," Dion said, resting a big hand on Numa's shoulder and squeezing. Her body warmed under his touch and she suppressed a shudder of need. There would be ample time for them to work on that task soon enough.

Neph's broad smile turned serious as he regarded Dionysus. "You're looking well, Father. I assume it's time to have a more serious conversation about the steps we need to take to do damage control with the humans of Meri's bloodline."

"We will," Dion said. "But not until we've gathered all the immortals here to discuss it, and that includes Deva."

Neph tensed and narrowed his eyes. Cade snorted from behind Numa, and she silently willed him to hold his tongue.

After regarding Dionysus for a moment, Neph finally nodded. "We will wait, but I admit I don't like the implications one bit. Deva's too young and inexperienced to be involved in the sort of thing I believe is required. I'd just as soon avoid involving her at all."

Beside him, Vrishti frowned. "She's a grown woman, and perfectly capable of making her own decisions. She's had so little control over her life so far. We owe her the respect due a fellow immortal. She is one of us, regardless of how new she is to the world."

"Agreed," Aodh said, causing the other men to look at him in surprise. "I may consider her a daughter, and have all the protective instincts that go along with that, but Deva is nothing if not strong-willed. It would be more dangerous to force a choice on her. She is in command of her own fate— we should allow her the chance to decide herself. I will support her no matter what."

"Then we shall wait," Neph said, giving his mates a grudging glance. "But I intend to remain cautious. I've assigned one of the Thiasoi to guard her while she's here. And whatever she decides to do, he will accompany her to ensure her safety."

"As long as you're not trying to control her life, I'm okay with that," Vrishti said. "She needs her freedom if she's going to be able to grow." She slipped beneath his arm and embraced him and they headed into the grand hall to greet Nyx and Nereus.

# CHAPTER 2

A shadow fell across the sun and Gavra opened his eyes, blinking up at the silhouette above him. It took a moment before he registered the shape as that of a man and not some wayward cloud, and the grin as Silas's.

"You're in my sun," he said, waving a hand in the air while he carefully cradled the bottom of the naked baby asleep on his chest.

"After a baby-shaped tan line, are you?" Silas asked. The sea breeze tossed Silas's thick, dark hair around his head as waves crashed in a lulling rhythm several yards from Gavra's feet.

Silas cocked his head playfully despite the dark circles under his eyes. His pheronesis had come on strong the day before, but with the baby's near constant need for care, it had been difficult to divert enough attention to Silas. Gavra had offered to take the baby for a few hours so Assana could tend to Silas for the afternoon. He looked much better than he had this morning, which was a relief. Perhaps they could get back to normal for the rest of the day until they left for the Haven.

Gavra's heart thudded hard. This feeling of complete domestic bliss was still somewhat foreign to him, even after a year of being happily mated. Add to that the past six months of basking in the presence of the tiny embodiment of the love he shared with his mates. Sylvanus looked more and more like his mother every day, and he could see the same adoration in Silas's eyes as he felt himself whenever either of them looked at the boy. Their son.

"Just a nap. Finally got him to settle down. How are you feeling?"

Silas shrugged. He viewed his quarterly fertile surges as a debilitating weakness. "Still teething?"

Gavra tilted his chin down to peer at the inert little lump sucking its thumb and drooling onto his sternum. He gently brushed a hand over the baby's head. "Horns came in . . . Can't tell yet whether they're satyr or dragon, though." He pulled his hand away from the pair of nubs when the baby squirmed. With a slow exhale, he wrapped a coil of red healing smoke around his son's crown and the baby gradually settled back to sleep, steadily sucking on his thumb once more.

Silas crouched down and leaned over with a hum of approval. "My money's on satyr horns. You know how much Assana cares about duty. She'd probably try to single-handedly replenish the satyr population if she could."

"There's no telling what a hybrid will look like. Probably no way to know for sure until he's older anyway. But I think you're right, at least based on the location. They're too far forward. Dragon horns are closer to the temples." To illustrate, he summoned his own horns, which erupted from the sides of his brow and coiled back, plunging into the warm sand behind his reclining beach chair.

Silas eyed the big protrusions, licking his lips. He let out a soft grunt and shook his head as if to clear it. "Put those away, dude. I don't need to be inappropriate in front of our kid." Shaking his head again, he stood and adjusted himself in his shorts, then shot a pained look at Gavra before turning to walk away.

Gavra chuckled. "They're almost as impressive as my dick, aren't they?"

"I don't know about that, but your dick needs to get it together. We've got to finish packing and head to the Haven soon. The in-laws want us there early."

Gavra sighed and glanced down to see a pair of vivid aqua eyes gazing back at him. With eyes like those, Sylvanus was definitely a satyr. "Ready to meet your granny, Syl?"

Sylvanus blinked and popped his thumb out of his mouth, offering it to Gavra.

He chuckled. "Might need that later when Nyx is monopolizing all of your mother's time. You, my boy, are going to have a sleepover with your cousins. How does that sound?"

The baby cooed and gurgled, then popped his thumb back into his mouth.

Gavra summoned a cloud of red that slipped around his body, condensing into a lightweight fabric sling that cradled the baby snugly to his chest. Getting up, he forced himself to shed the regret over leaving the idyllic island they'd called home for the last five months, ever since Assana's delivery.

The three of them had spent the first few months after the war ended taking a tour of the human world. Gavra hadn't mingled with humanity in thousands of years, and Assana had never even been outside the Haven. The youngest and most worldly of the trio, Silas was an eager tour guide, showing them all the wonders humanity had to offer, from technology to food to entertainment.

But after a life as quiet as the three of them were accustomed to, they soon longed to return to more solitary accommodations. So they'd chosen this remote island off the coast of Sumatra, close enough to the portals to their own worlds for them to travel quickly when needed, but far enough from humanity to avoid them if they chose.

The place they called home now had once been owned by a wealthy human who had either died or grown tired of it; Gavra wasn't really sure. All that mattered was the comfortable, rambling house with all its twenty-first century luxuries and the nearby ocean to remind Assana of home. Sylvanus had been born in that house, but it was time to introduce the boy to the rest of their kind before he got old enough to start believing his entire world was comprised of just him and his parents.

That, and Gavra ached for some solitary time with his mates that wouldn't be interrupted by a crying baby at the most inopportune moments.

Equinox had been tainted the year before by the deaths of so many of the higher races. It had been a bittersweet victory. This year they were reclaiming the day for its true purpose—celebrating life in the best way possible. Ideally that would mean doing nothing but fucking for the entire day. Silas certainly needed the undivided attention for a change.

As much as Gavra adored this life on the island, stolen moments with only one or the other of his mates while the third saw to the baby was getting old. He wanted them both in his bed again, and he meant to take advantage of the freedom the very second they dropped Sylvanus off in the Sanctuary and returned to the Haven. He gathered up his beach supplies and headed back to the house, eager to see what this year's Equinox would bring.

# CHAPTER 3

*A*urum patted the rich soil down around the tiny green seedling, then paused and sat back on her haunches, her earth-darkened fingers resting on her thighs. She took a deep breath of spring air and basked in the surrounding beauty. A warm afternoon sun shone down over the budding dogwoods and azaleas. The brilliant blue of the March sky stretched above the Black Mountain range, the trees tinged pale green from all the fresh growth awakening after a long Appalachian winter.

"I see why you came back here," she said, dropping her gaze to the human woman whose garden she was kneeling in.

Julia Proust smiled back at her. "It's home," she said. "Even when Alec and I were traveling, I couldn't deny the pull to return." She sent an adoring look down the hill to the big blond man maneuvering a riding mower around the grassy hillside.

"It's a good place to call home."

"Do you think the three of you will stay?" Julia asked, darting a glance at Calder and Nicholas, who were carefully stretching a new mesh shade cloth over Julia's arched green-house. Spring was in full force and the plants she grew for her nursery business needed sunlight more than shelter now. Julia and Alec had spent the past year helping Aurum and her mates acclimate to life in the small human town of Tuxedo Falls, North Carolina. It was the least Aurum, Calder, and Nicholas could do to repay the favor.

Aurum smiled warmly, admiring the two shirtless men who owned her heart and soul. "I enjoy being your neighbor, and I think the two of them are fitting in well enough. They deserve the freedom after all they've been through." She regarded Calder a moment longer, her teeth catching her lip with apprehension.

"They've definitely made an impression in town," Julia said. "And so have you with your baking. The town could do far worse. And now with Melody back with my granddaughter, it's really starting to feel like home again. But something seems like it's bothering you. Feel like talking about it?"

Aurum sighed and shifted down the row to dig her spade into the dirt for the next seedling. She glanced up at Julia, who looked back at her with faint concern in her lovely blue eyes shaded by the wide brim of her hat. "Nothing bad. It's just that we've been invited . . . or more like *summoned* . . . to return to the Haven for Equinox. I know it's supposed to be a celebration, but the place doesn't exactly hold happy memories for me."

Julia's lips tightened into a hard line and she dipped her head. Quietly, she said, "I heard about what happened. I may be selfish for saying this, but I'm glad Alec stayed out of it, even though he was torn by the decision."

The man on the mower caught them staring at him and grinned brightly. Julia beamed back, her aura flooding with pure joy that was as much from her natural state as it was from being mated to a Gold dragon.

"I don't blame you one bit," Aurum said. "But I fear I don't have the luxury of saying no. I can't keep Calder away from his family. The saving grace is that I think his mother might finally be a little more accepting of the fact that her son mated a dragon. She is family, whether she likes it or not, especially since my brother is mated to her daughter too." She snorted softly. "Though I have no doubt Gavra has kissed Nyx's ass enough to get back into her good graces already."

Julia laughed and bent back to her work. "I would love to meet the rest of your family one day. They sound amazing."

Aurum tilted her head thoughtfully. "You and Alec should come too. It's the best chance you'll get to learn more about the world you belong to, now that you're mated to a dragon."

Julia's face flushed crimson and she shook her head, her gaze remaining fixed on the hole she was digging that was already deeper than it needed to be. "Oh . . . I don't think I'd fit in . . ."

"You'll be among friends, and I promise we all have many varied interests. We aren't as hyperfocused on sex as you think."

"Speak for yourself."

Her gaze shot up to the dark-haired figure who stood at the end of the row. Nicholas grinned wickedly at her, his green gaze raking her hungrily. He held a large flat of seedlings in each arm and didn't even tear his gaze from her as he set them down.

"You should go, Mom," Melody said, arriving next to Nicholas and depositing the flat she'd carried up. "It sounds like the party of the year, and the Haven is definitely something to see. It's like the ultimate beach paradise and only opens four times a year."

Julia shook her head, setting her plant in the hole she'd dug. "No . . . I promised you I'd stay and take care of baby

Mora while you and the boys go. I want you to live your life, honey."

"You have a life too, Mom. Besides, we decided Mora needed to spend some time with other babies like her. Nicholas said we were welcome to take her to the Sanctuary. The ursa elders are watching the little ones for Equinox. She'll be fine."

Julia's brows drew inward as she stared down the hill toward the baby happily swaying in the bouncy swing set up on the back deck. Garen and Skye worked nearby, cleaning dead growth out of the flower beds near the house. "Babies like her . . ." She let out a long sigh that Aurum felt deep in her own chest. "I keep forgetting."

Aurum reached out and squeezed Julia's arm. "Your granddaughter is a dragon, Julia. It's all right to feel a little strange about it, but she does need to be with her kind as much as possible."

As if cued by the conversation, the drone of the mower ceased and Alec approached, his golden gaze fixed on Julia as he climbed the hill. When he stopped at the edge of the tilled dirt bed, he rested his hands on his hips. "We don't have to go if you don't want to, baby, but it is a once in a lifetime experience. One I haven't had since I was young. I'll tell you more while we get dinner started."

He held out his hand and Julia's aura spiked a brilliant pink. As if pulled by his simple gesture, she rose and carefully stepped over the rows of newly planted seedlings. Once Alec's arm was around her and they were headed back down the hill to the house, Melody let out a delighted giggle. "I guarantee no cooking's going to happen for at least an hour or more. So much for planting, huh?"

"Sun will be setting soon," Nicholas said, squinting at the sky. "We can still get these planted between the six of us." He turned, and with two fingers in his mouth emitted a piercing whistle. Both Skye and Garen turned their attention to him. Garen hooked the baby into his arm and jogged up the hill behind Skye, then deposited the infant on a nearby blanket. "We making this a team effort?"

Calder loped over from the greenhouse and surveyed the remaining work. "If we each take a row, we can have it done in a snap." He knelt on the blanket by the baby and cooed at her while Nicholas and Melody distributed the packs of seedlings down the rows to expedite the planting.

Aurum's womb ached at the sight of her satyr playing with the infant, and she caught Nicholas regarding her. She smiled up at him and offered a slight shrug. Over the past year, the urge to have another baby hadn't been as acute as it was now. She and Calder and Nicholas had returned to the small Appalachian town they'd escaped to in order to avoid Calder's angry mother's wrath. Nyx's sanity had returned with the end of the war, but the three of them were eager to leave behind the unpleasant memories of the Haven where they'd nearly died at the hands of their enemy.

The time they'd spent in the Stonetree family's house nearby had been some of the most joyful months in Aurum's long memory, and the three of them had found that joy once again in that house. She was grateful to Eamon and Edward and their children for offering the place to Aurum on a permanent basis. The only condition was that they take care of it and continue to take in any travelers going to or from the Sanctuary.

She'd found close friends in Julia and Alec, and in Julia's daughter Melody. And as it turned out, there were other neighbors who had been in the war as well.

Aurum glanced up at the sound of a truck engine approaching and wheels crackling over the gravel driveway. The engine turned off and two beautiful turul women hopped out. Anya and Vikki had fought beside them in the

Haven, and apparently were Julia and Alec's closest neighbors too.

Melody waved them over before they could head into the house. "Perfect! More hands to help!"

Anya crossed her arms and shook her head. "I knew we should've waited until sunset. Where're Julia and Alec?"

"Alec's busy explaining to Julia what Equinox in the Haven is like on a good year," Calder said. He shot Aurum a look. "The more dragon magic, the better. It'll finally feel like home again after this year, if all the races are there to celebrate."

The dark-haired, impish Viki bounced on her heels. "I can't wait! Only two more days. You all will be there, right?"

Aurum's reservations dissolved amid the enthusiasm flooding off all her friends in waves. She smiled back at the other women, then returned Calder's gaze with a silent promise of her own. "Wouldn't miss it for the world."

# CHAPTER 4

"I will never get tired of the sound of her voice."

Ked nodded in response to Marcus, filled with as much awe as his human mate. After a year of getting to watch Evie perform with her brothers' band, he still couldn't tear his eyes away. Her airy voice rose above the pitch of the dueling saxophones and she closed her eyes, holding the note from the last line of the song for several seconds while Ozzie's drum beat slowed. Beside Evie, Ked's sister harmonized into the microphone, Belah's richer, throatier dragon voice a perfect complement to Evie's delicate turul sound.

Ked darted a look to the side of the stage where Nikhil stood, dark gaze fixed on the band. His aura flared brightly at the end when the three targets of his attention turned toward him as if they were compass arrows aiming at true north. Belah smiled seductively at Nikhil, and both Lukas' and Iszak's gazes burned with the same intensity.

A flare of regret spiked into Ked's gut at the memory of all he'd done wrong at the start. His sister could have had Nikhil's love all along, if not for his foolish interference. But they were Fate's children, he reminded himself. Their paths had been drawn for them. Where they found themselves ulti-mately had been no accident, of that he was sure, but where they went from here was their choice. Sophia North had assured him of that.

"Fate has more pressing concerns than to micromanage your lives, now that you all have mates," Sophia had told him when he pressed her for information on his father's plans. He'd gotten no more detail out of her despite pushing into her mind with his power. The ancient turul seeress possessed surprisingly strong defenses.

It had been difficult to let go of his suspicions, but the past year had been refreshingly uneventful. It was a small blessing after the ordeal they'd endured together the year before since the most recent—and final—dragon ascension.

The previously enraptured crowd in the club roared with excitement when the song ended, everyone rising to their feet and clapping, whistling, and hooting. Ked and Marcus rose as a unit and joined in. Ked's heart thudded hard as Evie's gaze found his across the sea of cheering bodies. Sweet Mother, how he adored her. He reflexively reached out and tugged Marcus into his side. The other man gripped his waist with one hand while pumping his other fist in the air.

"Goddamn, I can't wait to be alone with the two of you," Marcus muttered, his words barely audible amid the din. Evie's turul hearing was beyond sharp enough to make out his words, though, and she blew him a kiss and winked. The crowd went wild anew as if the gesture was for them.

The band said their farewells and thank-yous and the stage lights dimmed.

"Come on," Ked said, grabbing Marcus by the hand and aiming for the door behind the stage. The crowd parted instantly for him as though repelled.

"It's fucking eerie how you do that so well," Marcus said.

"You could too, if you practiced using your powers at all."

"I'm done with that shit. I just want to be a man again, if it's all the same to you. Evie's mate. Sebestyan's father. Your fuck-toy."

Ked snorted and glanced back at Marcus as he pushed through the door. On the other side, he turned and slammed the door shut, pushing Marcus against it. Marcus grunted and let out a deep chuckle, already grabbing at Ked's neck in anticipation of the hungry kiss he planted on him.

"Likewise," Ked said, releasing the other man's mouth and licking his lips. He narrowed his eyes. "You taste like Evie. When . . . ?"

Marcus gave him a shit-eating grin. "I'm her fuck-toy too. She needed a stress reliever before going on stage. You were busy in a meeting with Belah and Nik, and it sounded too important to interrupt."

"Hm." Ked nodded. "We're expected in the Haven early. Tomorrow. Nik will drift us there at dawn."

"All of us? What about the Sebbie and Layla?"

"Sophia and Ozzie are taking them to the Sanctuary on the Equinox. All the babes will be watched and protected by the ursa elders. They'll be safe."

"Can you share why we need to show up early?"

"I would if I knew," Ked said. "Numa said it would be best to go over it all in person once we're there. She promised it wasn't a life or death situation, though, so you can relax."

Marcus expelled a breath. "Thank god for that. I imagine it's got something to do with Dion's power returning."

Ked stopped short halfway into the club's green room. He grabbed Marcus by the bicep and swung him around. "What do you mean? Numa didn't say anything about his power returning. How the hell do you know?"

"How can I not? I guarantee Nikhil knows just as well as I do. Surprised he didn't share as much with you in your *meeting*. We were both Meri's puppets and linked to the bloodline, which is Dion's bloodline now, and that blood is on *fire*. Of course it has the added side-effect of making you look even prettier than usual." He smirked and patted Ked's cheek. "As if you could look more fuckable."

Ked grabbed his hand and glared at him, then at the source of the soft snickers coming from inside the room.

"Am I right?" Marcus asked the others.

Evie bounded over and launched herself at them both. With synchronized ease, Ked and Marcus caught her, each with a hand at her waist as she hooked an arm around each man's neck.

"You're both the most fuckable guys on the planet." She pressed a quick kiss to each of their cheeks and beamed at them before sliding down again. Her slight body pressed tight against Ked's side and he resisted the urge to pick her up again and cradle her in his arms. Evie had grown tired of his babying her months ago . . . around the time she'd given birth to Sebestyan, in fact.

Ked caught the unamused looks of Evie's brothers as they cleared their throats. He met their stares and pulled Evie tighter against him, dipping his head to kiss her squarely on the mouth. She hummed against his lips, the benign sound of pleasure sinking into his ears and straight to his cock. The fuckers were well overdue for getting used to the idea of their sister having a dragon for a mate.

"Brother, please."

Ked reluctantly heeded his sister's exasperated objection, but couldn't resist darting a smug smile in the direction of her two turul mates. Iszak and Lukas looked pissed, but Nikhil chuckled and shook his head.

"We'll have time for all the fun in the world in two days' time," he said. "You can bet Evie's brothers and I will be taking advantage of it too. With *your* sister."

Marcus laughed, but Ked scowled. Finally he relaxed his

features and nodded. "Fair enough. Is Marcus right? Have Dion's powers returned?"

Nikhil's throat rippled as he swallowed, causing the glowing dragon mark that tied him to Belah to flare. He looked at Belah, who nodded. "Show him," she said.

"I don't know if we're all like this," Nikhil said. "Marcus will have to weigh in. But for the past two days, I've been able to pick any member of the higher races out of a crowd without effort. In the past, it always took quite a bit of observation and behavioral analysis. My Elites were all trained to learn the mannerisms of the different races, the cues that gave them away, but there were always a few who blended in well enough that we'd miss them. Not anymore. I can see them as clearly as if they had neon signs tacked to their foreheads. This is new, and I believe it's tied to the divine blood those of us who were once linked to Meri now possess. Come, I'll show you."

Ked followed him out the door to the shadowy corner at the back of the stage. The club's stereo was playing heavy blues, and the patrons danced just beyond. The bar was packed even after the final set ended, but there were still two hours until closing, and the music of Fate's Fools tended to keep the fans energized well into the night.

Marcus slipped up to Ked's other side. "You picking out the hidden dragons?" he asked under his breath.

"Dragons, ursa, turul. There aren't any nymphs out. The turul tend to blend in best with crowds like this, but your average human eyesight wouldn't know the difference without training. What do you see, Marcus?"

"I see a human woman about to get very lucky with a dragon and an ursa on the dance floor. Think they're together?"

"Where do you see that?" Ked asked, darting his gaze around at the swaying bodies in the flickering light of the club. He deliberately avoided using his power to pick out the figures, but could see several possibilities.

"Far left, near the bar," Nikhil said. "My guess is the dragon's a Gold and the ursa's a Sundance, judging by his coloring. All I see is how *different* they are. More vibrant. The magic clings to them. But even more troubling is that there are other humans who are starting to notice. Look at the bartender . . . He keeps giving them strange looks. I'd bet money that the bartender's linked to the bloodline too, and with the resurgence in Dion's power, he's able to see them for what they are."

Ked narrowed his eyes at the bartender and exhaled a breath. He silently commanded his power to seek out the higher races in the room and cloak them, beginning with the pair Nikhil had pointed out. His magic surreptitiously flowed through the shadows and clung to the dragon and ursa. The bartender blinked and shook his head, then shifted his attention back to the customers.

"This has potentially devastating consequences. I'm half tempted to leave for the Haven now."

"I recommend doing a bit of damage control first," Nikhil said.

Belah appeared at his side, her expression solemn. "Between the two of us, we can reach most of the higher races in New York," she said. "Come . . ."

She led them back into the dressing room and motioned for the others to gather around. Nikhil and Marcus stood back while Ked and Belah linked hands with Evie and Iszak to one side and Lukas and Ozzie to the other.

"Whisper the warnings into our breath," Belah said, then nodded at Ked. The two of them exhaled clouds of blue and black smoke that swirled into a misty sphere between them. The four turul barely moved their lips, but the message was clear as it filtered into the smoke: *Take heed, there may be danger of discovery among the humans. Retreat to seclusion until word comes that it is safe. Answers will come after Equinox.*

Then they commanded the cloud of smoke skyward. Ked followed the wisps as they faded to near nothingness and filtered into the air vents of the club to be distributed among the patrons and out into the night. Word would spread quickly, as it tended to now that the higher races were more closely bound.

"That should be enough to maintain order for now, at least," Belah said.

Marcus stepped back into the room and closed the door behind him while the rest of them settled into the sofas. "That place cleared out fast. Looks like it worked. Now what?"

"Now we make a toast to the end of an era," Ozzie said, grabbing a bottle of champagne out of the mini-fridge and holding it up. Everyone stared at him for a moment and he rolled his eyes. "I mean the band, not the whole goddamn world. I'm pretty confident that what we did was enough for now, but I'm gonna miss what we had here. A year was too little time to have you three back together just to have it end again so soon."

The blond turul's aura rippled with sadness and loss that was far more potent than this toast warranted, but Ked didn't know the man well enough to press for more details. He had the kind of broken-hearted aura of someone whose love was unrequited, which he'd never seen in an unmated turul before.

"The band's yours, if you want to keep it going," Iszak said, accepting a plastic cup filled with bubbly alcohol. "Fate's Fools doesn't need to die just because the three of us need to move on."

Lukas toasted his agreement. "Yeah, man. You were the

only thing keeping me and Iszak together all those years before we met Belah. You can rebuild it."

"You have our blessing," Evie said. "You can use it to play your song and finally find your One."

Ozzie sighed and rested back against the edge of a low cabinet strewn with the crumbs and half-eaten snacks from their intermission between sets. He took a swig straight from the bottle then set it on his knee, tightly gripping the neck. "I don't know if I see the point. What's Fate's Fools without you *fools*, anyway?"

"We weren't the only victims of Fate," Iszak said. "I guarantee if you put out the right ad, you'd have a slew of responses—dragons, ursa, and turul alike. Maybe even a nymph, if any of them are brave enough to venture out of the Haven. You've always been the glue, so I have no doubt you can pull it off again."

Across the room, Lukas strummed a guitar and burst into song, his clear voice ringing out over the thumping bass from the stereo in the club. "*Carry on, my wayward son . . .*" he sang, but Ozzie only looked even more forlorn.

"That isn't helping, dude. I'm gonna miss you fucks."

"Honey, we aren't dying," Belah said. "When the kids are older, we'll come visit."

The utterly downtrodden look on Ozzie's face made Ked feel like a ball of light by contrast. He didn't quite understand Ozzie's dark mood. The decision to raise Sebestyan and Layla in the turul Enclave hadn't been a secret. They'd talked about it off and on since the babies were born. The only reason they hadn't gone earlier was to give Evie a bit of time to enjoy her freedom, and for Ked and Belah to get a longer glimpse of twenty-first century human life up close.

"Nanyo's going to drive me batshit by the time the kids are out of diapers. Do you have any idea how hyperfocused that woman is on my love life?" Ozzie groaned.

Lukas idly strummed his guitar and started picking out a distinct tune again. Before Ozzie could object, Lukas scrunched up his face with faux emotion and belted out, *"Did you ever know that you're my hero . . . And everything I would like to be?"*

Ozzie lurched across the room and grabbed the guitar while Marcus doubled over in laughter. "Fuck you guys. I'll see you in the god damned Sanctuary after your party." With that, he stormed out of the room and slammed the door.

"That's my damned guitar!" Lukas bellowed. His shoulders shook with laughter. "Do you think we were too hard on him?"

"Well, the mood has lightened now that he's gone, and the fucking Void is still sitting right here," Iszak said, darting a look at Ked.

"He's been a mess all year," Lukas said. "You'd think he was in the thick of the fight last year, but all he did was hang out with Deva in the Realm of the Gods. It's as if babysitting was the worst thing in the world."

"He'll come around. It can't be easy to be the last man standing after watching all of us hook up," Evie said.

"Think he'll join in the festivities in the Haven?" Marcus asked. "He could find his One there, if he cared to try."

Belah shot him a knowing look and Ked shook his head. "Unlikely. If I didn't know better, I'd say your cousin is pining for love more than he's upset about losing you guys. When you go, he'll be losing the distraction from whatever the true hurt is that plagues him."

Iszak and Lukas both burst out laughing. "Not likely. He's been so keen on finding his One, we *know* he wouldn't shut up about it if it happened," Lukas said.

"Yeah, no fucking way," Iszak agreed.

Ked shrugged. "I'm just calling it as I see it."

# CHAPTER 5

The day before Equinox dawned, Deva rose to the sound of trumpeting dragon calls and laughter echoing around the Glade. She stepped out onto the vast perch that doubled as a balcony overlooking the empty sky and tilted her face toward the sun.

Blinking into the brightness, she squinted when she made out wings, then smiled when she realized that it wasn't the sun shining down on her, but her own mother. Neela's fiery wings blazed pale yellow against the sky and she twisted and swooped, calling out taunts to the massive and darkly iridescent dragon who flew after her. Zorion could barely keep up, and Deva laughed at the frustrated blast of flame that burst from his snout.

Deva's mother banked hard, her small form able to make tighter turns than her huge mate's. When she faced the perch, her eyes lit on Deva and brightened. She arced downward and came to a soft, graceful landing beside her daughter, rushing to pull her into a hug.

"Mom, you were so beautiful up there! I don't think I will ever get tired of watching you fly."

Neela's heat crackled against Deva's nightgown, but Deva had learned to hone her dragon resistance months ago just so she could hug her mother without fear of being burned.

"Oh shit," Neela said, jerking away and patting at the tiny flames that licked at the edge of Deva's clothing.

Deva laughed. "It's conjured. I can replace it."

"I know," Neela said, frowning. "I still need to learn better self-control. When I'm happy, I set things on fire. When I'm pissed, I set things on fire. It seems the only truly safe state with me is when I'm completely neutral, which is absolutely no fun at all."

Zorion's shadow swelled overhead, and he came to land with equal grace as Neela despite his size. The big dragon shifted and simultaneously split into two male shapes that clothed themselves with a breath. Zil's darker form dipped to kiss Deva on the cheek.

"Good morning, daughter. Are you well today?"

"I'm well enough. Ready for a change in scenery." She hugged him and his iridescent-skinned twin. As her mother's mates, she considered them her fathers, and felt more kinship with them than any of the other immortals in her family. The pair of unusual dragons were as sequestered as she was from the human world. But while she'd been kept close to her parents for her own safety, Zorion and Zil remained in the higher realms because their appearance made it problematic for them to blend with humans. She longed for more freedom to test the limits of her power and hoped that she could leverage the fact that tomorrow was her birthday to request a reprieve from the constant over-sight. She just didn't want to mention it in front of Zorion and Zil for fear of sounding insensitive to their situation.

But as always, Zorion seemed to know the inner workings of her mind. His expression softened and he cupped her cheek, the nacreous filaments of his veins lighting up within his arm. "You have been stifled for the past year, haven't you?"

"It isn't that," she said. "Well, it is partly that . . . but as much as each of the higher realms feels like home to me, I never feel *complete* when I'm in one place. I have this strange, surreal craving to . . . I don't know . . . *mash them all together.*" She held her hands up, palms facing, and mimed crushing something. "Is that crazy?"

"You want freedom." Neela shrugged as she shared an understanding look with Zorion. "Trust me, baby, I understand. If it were up to me, we'd all be out there exploring, but until I learn to rein in my fire and these two stop looking so fucking *godlike*, I'm afraid it isn't in the cards for us. But we have to wait for that. There's no harm in learning a little patience."

"I have been patient. I just don't think I have enough room to grow in the higher realms anymore."

She had restrained herself from yelling, but only barely. There was nothing to be patient about. She had mastered all the most basic skills of each element present within her blood. She could do all the spells in her sleep, from short drifts to conjuring clothing. She could even coax the most stubborn seeds to grow. And no one could deny that her singing was as beautiful as any turul's, and she'd become adept at playing just about every instrument she could get her hands on. The next level was within her grasp, the abilities so close she could taste that power, yet it eluded her.

"It will come with time, that's all," Neela said, though Deva sensed her mother's uncertainty.

She clenched her teeth. "All the signs point to my physical maturity being on schedule with at least being able to shift. I'm not going to get any better unless I challenge myself, which you guys won't let me do. My powers feel stunted . . . incomplete. I need to know where I belong to understand how they work, and as much as I love the higher realms, each of these places leaves me feeling unfulfilled . . . like I'm adrift without a clear purpose. I need more."

Deva stared between the three figures, hating their stricken looks. They didn't know any more than she did. Whatever she was, they were not equipped to understand how she worked.

A "chimera" they called her, but despite spending weeks in the Sanctuary libraries poring over ancient tomes supposedly written by gods, Deva could find no more than theoretical explanations of her nature. They claimed she had the potential for immense power, yet offered no discussion of how to tap into that power.

"I'm just tired of waiting," she sighed, then closed her eyes and drifted away.

The gut-twisting rush of that small bit of magic left her swaying with vertigo when she landed, and she nearly toppled off the edge of a cliff when a big hand grabbed her.

"Whoa there, kiddo. What's with the angry drifting?" Her uncle Naaz kept a tight hold on her arm, leading her down into the sunken living area of the cliffside house he shared with Deva's sister Asha.

The room swam and she crumpled onto their comfortable sofa, holding her head in her hands.

Deva groaned and accepted the glass of water proffered by a pale, delicate hand.

"Did my brother say something mean? I'm happy to go kick his ass," Asha said, settling beside her and rubbing her back while Naaz crouched in front of her.

Deva let out a rueful laugh and took a sip of water. "Just the same platitudes. 'It takes time, be patient.' I know I'm not strong enough yet, but I'm never going to *be* strong enough if

I don't test my boundaries." Looking at Naaz, she said, "How many people can you drift at once?"

Naaz lifted his brows and gave her a calculating look. "Well, it depends . . ."

"Dammit, I want a straight answer. Don't be diplomatic to avoid pissing off my parents. I'm honestly starting to believe it's a sex thing."

Naaz blinked and gave Asha a helpless look.

"What do you mean 'a sex thing'?" Asha asked.

Deva met her sister's wary gaze. "Please don't treat me with kid gloves, Asha. I need at least *one* ally here. Someone who understands what it's like to come into the world with three thousand years' worth of power and knowledge knocking around inside your brain. You were a virgin when Naaz woke you, yet that was no big deal."

"I'm going to go finish packing," Naaz said, practically running from the room. Asha moved to sit across from Deva on an oversized hassock and took her hands.

"I think I'm going to need you to elaborate just a little," Asha said.

"Everyone treats me like I might break if I start acting like a fucking adult. But I think I need more magic to reach the next stage in my training. Dragon magic. You know, the kind you get from fucking."

Asha's brows lifted and she smiled. "I see. But Deva, you are more than just a dragon. So much more. I know I didn't have a typical dragon childhood by any stretch, and yes, I was a virgin when Naaz and I mated. But I knew how things worked and was completely sure how to use my powers by the time Naaz awakened my body from hibernation. I'd had eons to mentally prepare. You're kind of the opposite."

Deva lifted her hands and let them drop to her lap in frustration. "That's where you're wrong, though. I remember every single second I spent in that tank Meri kept me in. Every experiment she did, testing new cocktails of blood in the infusions that kept me alive. It may have only lasted months, but there were eons of history carried in all that blood, especially in the satyr blood that sustained me for the entire time. And then when Vrishti became my mother . . ."

She stopped to swallow and shake her head, overcome by the memories that were still raw after a year. The room had gone blurry, but she could see that Naaz had crept back in and leaned silently against the sofa across from her.

"You remember all that?" Naaz asked, his voice gruff. The smudge of his aura flared with an old hatred.

Deva wiped her eyes and nodded. "Yes. I didn't think it would be productive to share that particular ordeal. It hurts just thinking about that vague memory of safety, then having it torn away. But I felt that safety again with Vrishti. And then when she changed just a few hours before I was born, I felt it even more—the Summer Spirit held me in her arms, cocooned me in her power for only a little while before I had grown too much to stay.

"Now I've outgrown the higher realms the same way I outgrew Vrishti's womb. Maybe not physically this time, but definitely mentally. I need more than this. And it isn't like I can just lie around and wait for my soul mate to come unlock my true potential. I don't have a soul, so I know that can't happen."

"Deva . . ." Naaz cautioned and she saw the hurt look on her sister's face.

"I'm so sorry. I know you didn't have a choice, but I'm feeling like I don't either, when I should, don't you think? If it had been in your power to go find *him*, wouldn't you have done that?"

"You bet your ass," Asha said, then sighed and squeezed

Deva's hands. "I know you're probably sick of hearing this, but please be patient. I know it's easier said than done, but coming from someone who had no choice in the matter, trust me, just give it a little more time. Don't force the issue or you'll wind up making a mistake."

Deva's shoulders sagged and she stared down at her sister's pale hands that stood out in stark contrast to her own darker skin. Vibrant multicolored fire sparked through the veins beneath Asha's skin, reminding Deva how much raw power her sister possessed. But her sister was also more than three thousand years old, while Deva was *technically* only a year old. In fact, the next day would be her first birthday. Which seemed completely absurd, because Asha looked the same age as Deva felt.

"What about the party?" Deva asked. "It's the Haven. I may not have joined in for any of the fun the nymphs like to have, but I *know* what goes on there on special occasions like this one. What's the point of me even going if my parents are dead set on keeping me from behaving like an adult?"

Asha regarded her with a careful look. Her rainbow gaze was one of the few features they had in common. She finally lifted a pale eyebrow and smiled. "Do you *feel* a need to dive into that kind of thing? Listen to your body. You already have the ability to recognize the magic when it clings to others. Like when I think of Naaz . . ." Asha closed her eyes and a small smile spread across her lips. Her aura flooded a deep crimson and she bit her lip. At the same time, the magic flowing through Asha's veins made her skin brighten to a more human shade and the brilliant tether that joined her soul to Naaz's lit up to the point that it almost appeared solid.

Deva studied her sister, her heightened senses able to pick up the increased pulse and the push of Asha's hard nipples against the snug top she wore. A sweet aroma filled the air, and a second later Naaz stood up straighter, his nostrils flaring and his brows drawing together. He stared between the pair of them for a beat, his own aura flickering with faint arousal tinged with uncertainty.

"Asha?" Naaz asked.

Asha opened her eyes and grinned at Deva, then glanced at her mate. "Just proving a point. We'll be ready to go soon."

Naaz left the room, shaking his head and adjusting his crotch. Asha bit her lip and lifted her eyebrows at Deva.

"See what I mean? Even just strong attraction can flood your body with power. But I get infinitely more power from Naaz than I would from someone I'm not bonded to."

Deva forced herself to shut off the part of her eyesight that saw those cues, particularly the brilliant magic that linked their souls. She'd never told anyone she could see their souls, once she learned it wasn't a common ability. But she'd become painfully aware over the past year of how powerful the bonds were between the souls of her family and their mates.

Everyone she loved had found their match and liked to throw around the words "soul mate" when they talked of their relationships. She firmly believed her lack of a soul was the thing holding her back, and no amount of physical, mental, or sexual awakening was going to give it to her.

Her throat tightened with frustration and sadness. "Asha, I don't know what I'm supposed to do. I know it's probably not sex that I need. It's a soul. But nobody knows how to fix me. I'm never going to have what you and Naaz have. Why should I even try?"

Asha pulled her into a hug. "Oh, sweetie. Stop thinking like that. You're a brilliant, beautiful, talented person. There's bound to be a place for you somewhere. Spend some time with Dion after tomorrow's party and pick his brain. He might have some ideas."

Deva sniffled and wiped her eyes again. Her family was nothing if not caring and understanding most of the time. Perhaps Asha was right—she could take advantage of the wealth of power and knowledge her various aunts and uncles shared. She had immortals among the ten individuals who she called her parents. Someone was bound to have some ideas to help her push to the next level in her power, even if they couldn't help with her other problem.

There was only one person who her instincts told her could help with that. One man who had ever made her body respond the way Asha's did at the mere thought of her mate. Yet she didn't know if she could find the courage to even utter his name to catch his attention. Because despite her ache for Ozzie West, he had only ever looked at her like a child, and had only ever touched her like a woman in her dreams. How could she confess to him that she believed he was her answer to finding a soul? She supposed she wouldn't really know unless she tried, and the Haven's festivities might be her best chance to get him alone.

She took a deep breath and released Asha from the desperate hold she had on her hands.

"Feel better?" Asha asked, studying Deva's face. "Your aura's brightened with purpose. It looks good on you."

"Yes. I am going to see what I can learn in the Haven. No more brooding."

"I'm always here for you if you need me," Asha said. "Naaz too."

"Thank you for not babying me like my parents do," Deva said. "I needed that."

"We all love you and want you to be happy. But don't let their cautious nature stop you from going after what you want. You can trust your instincts too."

Deva smiled and stood. "I will. Are you guys ready to go?"

Naaz entered the room again with two satchels slung

over his shoulder. After Deva drifted to her own room to collect her things, she met them in the center of the Glade where they waited for the others.

Deva relaxed, relieved to have even a glimmer of a purpose, no matter how unrealistic it might be.

# CHAPTER 6

*E*nergy was high in the Haven when they arrived, the place inundated with excitement. In the great hall, Deva found the rest of her throng of parental units together. Ever vigilant, Nikhil was the first to spy their entrance, and she and Asha rushed into his outstretched arms.

Deva adored all her fathers, but there was something about this severe, often frightening man that endeared him to her more than the others. Despite being her biological father while the others were merely the mates of her three mothers, she hadn't met him until well after the war had ended and the Haven was declared safe for her to return to from the Realm of the Gods.

Nikhil doted on both her and Asha in a way none of her other fathers did. She recognized the love in all their auras, so there was no mistaking how they felt, but Nikhil always hugged her with a ferocity that suggested he would move mountains for her happiness if she asked.

"My beautiful daughters," he said, releasing them and touching their cheeks with each of his strong hands.

"I missed you, Daddy," Deva said, her heart swelling with

love. "I wish I could have visited you in New York. You should come to the Glade more often."

"You can come see us more often soon," Belah said, slipping in beside Nikhil. "We're moving to the turul Enclave after Equinox. It'll be safe for you there."

Deva bit her tongue, grateful for Asha's interruption to say hello to her mother before moving on to greet the others. Deva's safety had always been their chief concern, which she'd understood, but it had gotten old.

"I would like that," she said, though she couldn't snuff the tiny spark of resentment at the reminder of her need to be kept "safe"—from what, precisely, was still unclear. There had been mention of a vague threat of their old enemy still remaining, even though the head had been severed from the proverbial snake a year ago.

The mention of the turul Enclave reminded her of her mission and she glanced around the massive hall, now thronged with nymphs and ursa who had arrived a day early in anticipation of the party to come. Iszak and Lukas beckoned with a whistle, and she went to greet them with quick pecks to their cheeks. Of all the men she claimed as parents, they were the least overbearing—she guessed it was in deference to Nikhil, who likely did the bulk of the worrying for the three of them.

"I wrote a new song!" she exclaimed when she pulled back. Music was her greatest joy, unlike any of the other skills she'd attempted to perfect over the past year, but it wasn't as though it were a power . . . not like the way her turul fathers could harness the wind and lightning in a fight, or so she'd heard.

Iszak's eyebrows lifted and Lukas grinned. "Excellent! Let's hear it," Lukas said.

Deva darted another glance around the room, wondering where the true target of her new song could be, but Ozzie was nowhere to be seen. Tamping down her disappointment, she took a deep breath and launched into the song. The room fell completely still as the words and notes floated into the air, an almost melancholy ode to her sequestered life and the longing for more outside the shelter she had within the worlds of her birth.

She got to the final verse, but rather than sing it, she carried the last note a few moments longer and stopped. That last part had been written with Ozzie in mind, and she couldn't bring herself to sing the complete song without him listening. Was it foolish of her to adore the man so completely? Probably. But she couldn't help it. Her earliest memories were of Ozzie's voice easing the pain of her transformation from a child into a woman, and the singing helped her forget her lack of control over her life. He'd been there for her during the most frightening part of her life but had been disappointingly absent since.

When she grew silent and took a small bow to the gathered crowd, everyone cheered.

"Sounds like your turul side is blossoming," Lukas said. "That was beautiful, Deva."

"Thank you," she said softly and hugged him. She let out a deep sigh into his shoulder and blurted out the question she longed to know the answer to before she could chicken out. "Where's Ozzie?"

Lukas and Iszak shared a pained look. "He's not coming to the party this year. I'm afraid he's holding a grudge over us leaving the band. Evie too."

Deva's heart fell. "Oh . . ." she said lamely, and was about to make some useless excuse for her disappointment when a booming voice carried through the room, calling for the Quorum of Immortals to gather in the council chamber for business. What business could they have besides tomorrow's party?

"That means us too, brother," Iszak said. "See you later."

Deva smiled after them as they filed through a big door at the back of the room along with all her other parents and aunts and uncles.

When the doors closed, Deva slipped around the room, accepting warm greetings from the nymphs and ursa she had befriended over the past year. Several dragons and humans clustered together, and she recognized the group as the Court dragons and their mates.

The back of her neck prickled when she paused to take advantage of the table of refreshments that had been laid out along one long wall of the great hall. Glancing behind her, she caught the gazes of the four Thiasoi satyrs who stood to one side engaged in low conversation. Nymphs hovered around the edges of their group, subtly seeking attention, and Deva felt all the more conspicuous for having captured it.

One of the satyrs broke away and approached her. Her heartbeat quickened and she fumbled the pastry she held, then put it down, plastering on a smile to cover her nerves when the big man stopped and bowed deeply in front of her, his luxurious, dark waves falling over his handsome face.

"Lady Deva," he rumbled. "I am Llyr." When he stood again, he reached out and took her shaking hands in his and bent over her knuckles, kissing the back of each hand softly. "You don't remember me, do you?"

"I . . . can't say that I do," she said, even though it was a blatant lie. She couldn't have identified any of the four Thiasoi by name, but she felt the link to them all thrum in her veins. Which was what made it so damn difficult to even look this one in the eyes.

"Come walk with me." He kept hold of one of her hands, gesturing with the other to one of the arched doorways that led out of the great hall into one of the many ornamental water gardens that surrounded the palace.

Something about his bearing, with his head dipped slightly in deference, gave Deva a sense of value she rarely felt among her parents and extended family. The light squeeze of his hand sparked a tiny flame of rebellion and amplified her wavering confidence. She smiled up at him and nodded. "A walk sounds wonderful."

Llyr kept hold of her hand as they strolled around the bridges and vine-covered platforms that arched and twisted around the water garden. The Source-infused water flowed around moss-covered rocks forming small waterfalls that meandered among reeds and papyrus. His palm was warm and dry against hers, and the longer he held her hand, the more conscious she became of the intimacy of the contact. She couldn't decide whether to be elated or frightened. This was something lovers did—holding hands. Did he want to be her lover? Did she want to be his?

Eventually he paused in one of the few sunny patches of the misty garden and turned to her.

"I was with you from the beginning, as were my brothers and Nereus. My brothers and I have longed to speak to you since we came home, but it never seemed the right time, and things are more complicated now than when we were captured and imprisoned."

Deva nodded. "I owe you my life."

Llyr smiled and shook his head. "I wouldn't go that far. It's true that our blood fed you when you were growing in Meri's lab, but none of us had a choice. That isn't to say we wouldn't have given freely, had we been offered the choice . . ."

A thought occurred to her and she snatched her hand away from his as if it had burned. "Does this mean you are . . . that I am part you? Them?"

Llyr's mouth opened slightly and his brows rose in shock. "No. Calder hasn't been able to identify all the sources of the genetic material Meri created you with, but he knows your nymphaea side comes from Nereus, not any of us. It's ... ah ... it's all right to hold my hand."

Deva frowned. "But I do still carry some of your blood. That doesn't just disappear."

"And it never will, which is what makes this tricky for me and my brothers. We didn't want to overwhelm you, so agreed that only one of us should come to you."

Deva's heart was in her throat as she stared up into his deep aqua eyes. "Come to me for what?" she whispered, already well on her way to imagining how she and Llyr might spend the rest of the day. She could forget about her parents and Ozzie all at the same time.

"To offer my loyalty and my sword." He speared her with an earnest look and Deva gasped as he dropped to one knee. "I would serve as your guard, as a daughter of Neph. My body is yours, if you will have me."

Deva blinked in confusion. "Your . . . sword? You just want to be my guard? I thought you meant . . . Oh, shit." She covered her face with her hands and shook her head, mortified by the misunderstanding. She wanted to turn and run, but stood rooted to the spot.

"Deva?" Llyr gently grabbed her wrists with his big hands. "Look at me. What are you afraid of? Your fears are my duty to vanquish."

"Please stand up," Deva choked out.

He obeyed, and if she hadn't been aware of his immense size and rippling physique before, she was hyperaware of it now, particularly how much of it was on display. The flimsy sarong that twined around his waist left nothing to her imagination.

*My body is yours . . .* Holy shit, had she misinterpreted *that* declaration.

"Deva . . ." His deep voice sounded strained. "You know that we share a blood meld. It is limited, but it allows me a link to your thoughts, your emotions, if I take advantage of it. Sometimes I can't help but catch glimpses of what you feel."

Her eyelids flew wide open and she gaped at him. "Even just now . . . ? Oh my god, I didn't mean to . . . you're just so *big* and . . ." She groaned, then bent over the railing with her face in her hands again.

Llyr leaned down beside her, his shoulder brushing against hers. "The best thing to do is just say what you're thinking. I can handle honesty. I am also happy to give you any answers you desire."

"You work for my father. Aren't there rules against being too . . . ah . . . intimate with me?"

"There are rules against taking advantage of a situation. But there are no rules against being your friend. I made a promise to Neph that I wouldn't use our link for my own pleasure. But the link puts me in the best position to be your protector."

"Why you and not one of the others . . . or all of you?"

Llyr gave her a sideways smile. "Guarding you is a commitment. We're the last living unmated satyrs in the Haven. If we were all dedicated to your welfare, a *lot* of nymphs would take issue with that."

Yet again, Deva's mouth opened in shock and she immediately shut it again, still staring at him. "You're giving up mating to do this? That doesn't sound fair."

"I'd lose the link to you if I blood melded anyone else. It is an honor, trust me. My brothers all wanted the job as much as I did, but we knew only one of us could have it. It is a small price to pay to give you more freedom."

*More freedom.* The thing she ached for more than anything, that she was also certain would help her push her limits and strengthen her power. Her initial disappointment at the formal nature of his role disappeared and she grabbed his hands. "With you I'll be allowed to go into the human world finally?"

"We'll need to be cautious at first, but yes. Your parents didn't already tell you?" His face darkened and he grimaced. "Fuck. Tomorrow's your birthday. I probably just spoiled the surprise, but I couldn't wait to talk to you."

She let out a soft snort. "I'm always the last to know anything that has to do with me, birthday present or not. I get the sense they're still trying to figure out how to help me, but all I want is to have the freedom to figure things out on my own. For all I know, they're in that room right now talking about *me* instead of whatever Haven business is on the table right now. I almost can't believe they'd do this."

Llyr gave her an odd look, and her stomach flip-flopped when he grabbed her hand. "We need to go in. You're absolutely right. I can't believe they'd do this either."

"What? What did they do?" She let him lead her back the way they had come.

He shot a glance over his shoulder and she gasped at the swirling maelstrom of power in his eyes. "You might not be powerful enough yet to safely leave the higher realms alone, but you are damn sure mature enough to be involved in the decisions they make for you. You should be in that council chamber now, Deva. You're every bit the immortal they are."

"Party planning isn't really my thing," she said when they reached the grand hall again and he stopped in front of the enormous translucent glass doors that led to the council chamber. "Really, it's all right."

"You think they're just talking about how many orgies to have tomorrow? How many babies need to be conceived during the fertility rites? It isn't about that, and I've heard your name tossed around enough between them to know you're a frequent topic. I thought you knew already, but if you don't, you need to."

He pushed the doors open and stepped aside to give her access. Several voices clashed in an argument and Deva recognized Nikhil's angry baritone along with Neph's and Aodh's as they faced off around the table near the front of the room. The three fathers she was closest to stood their ground against Dionysus, who loomed at the head of the long council table.

"It is absolutely out of the question!" Nikhil yelled. "Deva is too young and inexperienced to be arbitrarily volunteered for some sex ritual. Someone else must do it. Hell, I'll do it!"

She was stunned by the instant validation of Llyr's warning. How long had they been talking about her?

Beside Dion, Nyx raised her head and met Deva's gaze. She lifted a hand and the buzz of voices ceased. "Perhaps Deva would like to weigh in herself," Nyx said, and all eyes turned toward her.

Llyr rested a hand on her shoulder and squeezed. "I've got your back, Deva," he said.

Steeling herself for the confrontation, she continued forward to the foot of the table where Lukas and Iszak stepped aside to give her room. They both wore frowns that suggested whatever was being discussed was just as distasteful to them as it was to her other fathers.

Pressing her palms to the cool tabletop, she took a deep breath and glanced around at all the expectant faces. Her family, her friends, all looked back—some worried, some sympathetic. None of their expressions made sense.

Finally her gaze rested on Nyx. Her aunt was the only one here who seemed willing to give her room to speak. "Do you mind explaining what all this is about?" Deva asked.

All at once a dozen voices rose, clashing and echoing through the room. Irritated, Deva took a deep breath. "Quiet!" The exclamation left her lungs with an odd warmth, as though it weren't a mere word, but crafted from dragon fire, even though no flames passed her lips. But it worked. The room fell dead silent and she tried again.

"I would like Nyx to tell me what's going on. If the rest of you will kindly let her, I would appreciate it."

Her aunt nodded. "We have a bit of a dilemma which we believe you are the solution to, but it seems you have a very passionate collection of overprotective parents who are objecting to the idea of you being involved at all." Nyx speared Neph—one of the so-called passionate, overprotective parents—with a stern look. "To the degree that they refused to even invite you in, as though the argument were entirely moot and we could solve the problem without you. I'm glad you're here so we can get this out of the way."

With that, Nyx tilted her head to Dionysus. "My father will explain the core issue."

Dion's deep voice filled the room, part thunder, part silk, and Deva was comforted by the return of Llyr's hand on her shoulder keeping her grounded in the face of the god's renewed power.

"You are only one of millions who share my bloodline, Deva. With the return of my power, the humans linked to me will soon possess the ability to recognize members of the higher races without effort. We must keep our secret. To do that, we need to reach those humans, which is no simple task."

"And you think I can help?" Deva asked. Her body tingled with the fresh possibilities that might be on offer with this discussion.

Dion nodded his big horned head. "We believe you are the *only* one who can help."

Nikhil lurched out of his seat. "Bullshit! She is innocent, inexperienced. She's existed in our world for only a year. I will *not* allow her to be part of this!"

"Stop!" Deva yelled, again surprised by the power that seemed to infuse her lungs and her voice, and how it led to Nikhil's instant subdual. "Please let me hear everything. Let me decide for myself. Dionysus, why do you think I'm the only one who can do this?"

"Because of your nature. The humans attached to my bloodline possess a varied set of mutations due to Meri's ancient experiments with the blood of the higher races. There are some with dragon blood, some with ursa blood, quite a few with satyr blood, and others with turul blood—or any mix of the four. You are the only one here with a perfect balance of all five races running through your veins."

Nikhil scowled and sat back, muttering to himself and crossing his arms. Dion shot a look at him and held up his hand. "What's more important is that you were *born* this way. There are few moments more powerful than the crossing of a threshold. In a female's life, there are three incredibly powerful thresholds that get crossed—leaving her mother's womb, the moment when she loses her virginity, and the moment she first gives birth. All parties involved in those crossings are affected. When you were born with this mix of blood in your veins, it rendered you uniquely suited for this purpose, among others. No other creature in this room can claim that."

Deva took a deep breath, slowly starting to grasp the implications of the problem. "But I barely have any power. I can conjure you a hat, but I can't even breathe fire yet."

"You won't need to use magic to help us," Nyx said. "And contrary to Nikhil's objections, you won't be required to participate in any of the individual fertility rites."

"What do I need to do?"

"As the apex of the ritual to reach the bloodline, you will act as a conduit to allow a message to reach them. Nothing more," Dion said. "The rest of us will provide the magic to power the message and the charm that goes with it. The waters of the Haven will carry the magic to you at the Source. From the Source's waters, you should be able to channel sufficient power from all of us to link to the entire bloodline, to speak to those dormant parts of each human that possesses the blood of any of the higher races, and to transmit the message they need to hear."

"What is the message, exactly?"

"I will tell it to you before the ritual begins. To put it simply, we will be imparting understanding to these humans about the higher races. If they discover our existence any other way, we would have to kill them, and that is not the ideal solution. Instead, we will provide an image that answers all their questions, offers our protection, and compels them to secrecy. If the power is strong enough, we will also encourage them to swear loyalty to the higher races, but that will remain up to you."

Deva's skin tingled with the prospect of having a role to fill for once. Her throat tightened with the most potent desire she'd ever experienced—the desire to have a true purpose. Even if she didn't use her still limited powers, she could help in a way no one else in the room could.

"When do we start?" she asked.

# CHAPTER 7

*D*eva fended off mental exhaustion the next day as she made her way to the Source with Llyr at her side. She'd spent the previous evening in the council chamber with Dionysus and Nyx coaching her through the process of linking to the bloodline and transmitting the message.

Neph's and Nikhil's protests hadn't ceased, and finally she'd asked everyone to leave, which had been one of the hardest things she'd ever done. But their world depended on her now. Couldn't they see that?

Only her uncle Naaz remained, along with Naaz's closest friends, Marcus and Sterlyn. They were to be her test subjects for delivering the message. As humans who'd endured Meri's experiments, all three men were part of the bloodline.

Llyr also insisted on remaining by her side, for which she was grateful. And now he would coach her through the ritual, serving as a barometer for the amount of power that would be flooding through the waters of the Haven soon, and the telepathic link between her and all the participants.

Each of the immortal dragons and their mates would be stationed at different locations throughout the Haven. Deva had seen the elaborately decorated pavilion at the edge of one of the many waterfalls that cascaded down the Haven's worn stone grottos. The main festivities would happen there, where Dionysus and his mates would hold court. But it was Deva's aunt Numa who was the key—as a dragon, Numa was better equipped to absorb her mates' sexual energy and channel it through herself into the Haven's water.

This was why each of the six immortal dragons had spread out around the Haven, so they could each do the same if and when their power was required. All Deva had to do now was wait. When the first wave of magic reached her, it would be time to begin. It would be up to Llyr to anticipate her needs and communicate with the others if she required more power to complete the task.

She paused at the edge of the rippling pools of the Source, staring down at her wavering reflection. The Silas tree towered above, its high branches lost in the mist where it penetrated the border between the Haven and the Sanctuary, standing sentinel over the Sanctuary's central lake. Around and beneath the surface of the Source's pools, the tree's roots extended in an endless tangle, so it appeared to float rather than being embedded in actual earth. The roots created endless ledges and steps that were tricky to navigate without slipping, and she struggled to stay dry as they approached the center.

"Only a little farther," Llyr said, touching her elbow gently.

Deva took a deep breath and stepped into the water, wading slowly deeper, her gown floating up around her waist like a billowing cloud. She wore no undergarments and was suddenly self-conscious in front of the big satyr who followed close, but when she glanced back at him, he merely smiled and nodded.

"You've got this," he said.

The pool they crossed wasn't large, but it was deep, and soon the bottom fell away and she had to swim the last few feet to the small island of roots that surrounded the trunk of the tree.

She reached the tree and grappled at the twisted roots to haul herself out of the water. Llyr hoisted himself out and took her hand, easily lifting her the rest of the way.

"Thank you," she said, wringing out her dress. She inhaled sharply and turned away from the big man when she realized her bodice was soaked through to her skin and nearly transparent.

"We both need to keep our feet in the water," Llyr said, wandering a few yards around the tree. "This pool looks better. There are roots to sit on under the water and it isn't as deep . . . Are you all right?"

Deva glanced over her shoulder, nodding as he pointed at the perfect ledge of roots that twined together about a foot beneath the water close to the tree trunk. "I see, thank you." Then she went back to brushing and plucking ineffectually at the wet fabric that covered her breasts, in a near panic because it wouldn't dry.

Llyr called her name again. "We need to get into position. What's wrong?"

He gripped her upper arm and moved around to her front.

"Don't!" Deva cried, twisting away and covering herself protectively.

He stared down at her with a frown. "Are you hurt?"

"No, it's just . . . my dress is wet. I don't want you to see."

"See what?"

Heat flooded her face and she shook her head. "Just don't look at me."

"You were just swimming. Of course your dress is wet. If you wanted to avoid that, you should have taken it off. Here . . . I can fix it."

He reached for her arms where she had them protectively caged across her breasts and pried them open. Deva clenched her eyes shut, waiting for some kind of reaction, but none came.

"You don't need to be afraid," Llyr said in a gentle voice. "Your beauty is nothing to be ashamed of."

"I'm not ashamed. I'm just . . . not used to . . . this." She lifted her gaze and gave him a defiant look.

Llyr raked a hand through his inky black hair and laughed. "This? You are part nymphaea, Deva. And part ursa, I might add. Being naked in mixed company is no oddity for shifters like us. It's something we grow accustomed to from an early age. Dragons are the only ones who are addicted to clothing, but even most of them don't mind running around naked in the right environments."

"Then why aren't you naked now?"

He lifted a shoulder and let it drop. "Because you seemed to have trouble focusing yesterday when I was wearing less than I am now. I thought being naked might be too much. It's my responsibility to protect you, not distract you. You are my charge, not the target of my seduction."

With a glance at his hips, she realized that he was indeed wearing a sarong that was more opaque than the one he'd been in the day before, though the rest of his toned and muscular body was pleasingly on display—and glistening wet now, to top it off.

"Now, do you want me to dry you off, or can you deal with the exposure?" He dropped his eyes to her chest and smiled. "Because you really may as well be naked."

Her nipples pricked and she slapped her hands back over her breasts, face blazing almost as hot as the flames that licked through her lower body in response to his frank appraisal of her.

"Dry me, please."

He nodded. "Move your hands."

She obediently dropped them and waited. Llyr stepped closer and lifted his hands to her shoulders. "I need to touch you for this to work, all right? When I'm done, your dress will be as dry as I can make it, though I think it's pointless."

Deva swallowed and nodded, her pulse racing at his proximity. He squeezed her shoulders gently and began to lower his hands, flattening them along her collarbone and moving down.

"You're not just doing this to cop a feel, are you?" she asked, voice shaking.

His lips twisted and his eyes twinkled. "You did give me the perfect excuse, but no, I genuinely need to be in contact to absorb the moisture from your dress. See?"

He lifted one warm palm from the front of her chest just at the edge of her bodice, and she glanced down. The soft white fabric where his hand had been was bone-dry. Her eyes widened.

"That's amazing! Can you teach me to do that?"

"Sure, but after we take care of this task." He slid his hands lower and Deva gasped at the sudden warmth that covered her breasts. Her nipples ached beneath his palms and Llyr's brows twitched briefly, his aura spiking red for a split-second before he moved on, sliding his hands down her stomach. He left behind dry cloth covering hot skin, and when he dropped his hands to his sides again, Deva mourned the loss of contact.

He stepped back and waved his hands in a little flourish.

"All dry. Well, except for the hem, but you're kind of standing in a puddle."

"Thank you," she said with a hesitant smile. "I'm sorry I'm such a pain."

"Nonsense. We need you to be as free from distractions as possible for this. Are you ready? The others are waiting for word from us before they begin."

Deva spun to face the tree and surveyed the tangle of roots near the pool Llyr had indicated. She finally found one big root that jutted up enough to provide a rudimentary bench for her to rest on. The water from the Source moved in a constant flow beneath and within the tree, emerging in a cascade over the tops of the roots. She sat on the wet root with her feet still dangling in the water, feeling ridiculous for worrying about her dress now that she had no choice but to let it get drenched again. At least the part that covered her breasts was dry now.

She settled down and hiked up the hem to her knees so the wet fabric didn't wind up tangled around her feet if she needed to move. Then she leaned back against the rough tree trunk and closed her eyes.

Inhaling deeply, she worked to center herself and focus on the core of power within her. She'd learned to recognize the five different aspects of her energy and had hoped that with gentle nurturing they would grow, but they still remained small and dim, like dormant seeds waiting for the rain and sun. Perhaps this task would infuse her with enough magic to kick-start her true power.

Reaching out, she could feel the bloodline, but at the moment it only consisted of the few individuals in the Haven who were linked: Nikhil, Marcus, Sterlyn, and Naaz, as well as her dragon father, Aodh, whose tie to it was faint. Her mother Neela had once been part of it, but when they'd tried to link to her, there was no sign of the bloodline to be found.

They concluded that Zorion's dragon fire had burned away the taint of Meri's blood when he brought Neela back to life as a phoenix the year before.

Deva hoped that by the end of the ritual, Nikhil would relax a little. With Llyr as her companion and guardian, she finally had an excuse to spend time in the human world without worrying about the potential dangers that probably were all in her parents' heads. And if they weren't, this message she was about to send should solve the problem.

At the sound of splashing, she opened her eyes to see Llyr hop over a thick root and settle down on a lower one in front of her with his feet in the water on either side of hers. "Are you ready?" he asked. "Dionysus and Numa will begin the ritual. At any point if you need anything, you tell me, all right? If it's less power, more power . . . anything."

"All right. Just make me one promise."

"Ask away."

"Don't ever shut me out to try to protect me. Especially not during this. I know I'm inexperienced, but I can't test my limits with everyone erecting walls around me. If you think I need to push myself, I will—I can handle it."

Llyr lifted his eyebrows and smiled. "I'm going to hold you to that. Especially after your meltdown over a little water. Getting naked is part of who we are, you know. And what you're about to start feeling when they begin the ritual is also who we are. You are all of these things, Deva . . . It's fine for you to want to take your time exploring your identity as a new breed of immortal, but don't lose sight of all the individual parts, because they are all amazing."

"I think as long as I have you to coach me, I'll figure it out. Thank you. You can let them know I'm ready now."

"Good."

# CHAPTER 8

The lattice of twisted vines that made up the roof of the new pavilion cast crisscrossing shadows over the pool beneath it. Numa surveyed the throne on the platform in the center that seemed to float on the water's surface, boasting a wide walkway leading from the courtyard below. The immense chair had a high back and wide arms woven from more vines and was big enough for the god who sat upon it now. The vines twisted around each other, providing numerous hand-holds to facilitate a multitude of configurations for the throne's true purpose. A shiver of pleasure cascaded through Numa at the very idea of what was to come very soon.

Dionysus idly observed his surroundings, though Numa sensed the vigilance in his body and aura. He could have just as easily been awaiting battle as an orgy. Her other mates loitered around the outer edges, waiting for the signal for the start of the festivities, all of them as eager to begin as she was.

She moved to the edge of the platform and dipped a toe in, kicking up a splash of water that hit Cade square in the face. He surged through the water with a growl, his fierce gaze tinged with salacious promise.

"It isn't time for that yet," Numa cautioned when he reached her and snatched at her legs. She hopped back with a giggle and fell against Dion's knees, and he slipped his arms around her and pulled her onto his lap. Numa managed an unconvincing protest, then gave in, sighing at the sensation of his lips along the side of her neck.

"It's time now," Dion rumbled against her ear. He yanked at the front of her sheer gown until the fabric tore, her breasts spilling out.

Numa wiggled against him. "Are you sure?"

Dion's teeth grazed her throat as he palmed her breast, squeezing and tweaking her nipple. With his other hand he cupped her chin and tilted her head, granting himself better access to tease his tongue along the edge of her jaw.

"Yes. Llyr has confirmed that Deva is ready. Let's make sure the first wave of power is potent enough for her to reach the entire bloodline. But even if it isn't, we have all day to try."

Numa felt like a doll in the god's grasp. She'd missed his immense size over the past year. Reaching back, she clung to his neck, arching into his touch as he tore her gown completely off and lifted his head.

With a deep, bellowing voice that made her core clench, he yelled, "The ritual begins! Rejoice and take your pleasure, nymphs and satyrs, ursa and dragons and turul. Enjoy the fruits of each other's desire, and come drink of the power when you thirst!"

"The wine is not in this pavilion, you know this, right?" Numa asked, gasping as Cade slipped down to his knees in front of Dion's throne and took her nipple into his mouth.

Dion shifted his hips up and gripped one of her thighs to reposition himself. She glanced down to see his cock in

Zeph's hands, the West Wind's tongue sliding up and down the shaft.

"Wine isn't the refreshment I'm offering, little one," Dion said.

Her gaze fixed on Zeph's lips where they wrapped around the thick head of Dion's cock. The god slid his fingers up her thigh and parted her slick folds, toying with her clit with idle flicks.

She let out a sigh and clutched at Cade's head, her gaze flickering with the heat of pleasure and enjoyment at the sight of Bekim and Theron, who each slipped into place at the rear of the two men kneeling closer to the throne. Cade grunted at the swift penetration of Bekim's cock into his ass, but resumed his sucking and licking at her breast as if this were a normal occurrence.

Zephyrus shifted positions and rested his knee atop Dion's thigh to give Theron access. The bearded ursa went to his knees behind Zephyrus first, dipping his head to suck the West Wind's balls into his mouth before teasing his tongue between his cheeks until he was forced to release Dion's cock with a gasp of pleasure.

"I see," Numa said. "You're going to let all the revelers drink directly from the source, are you? Straight out of the bottle itself?"

She reached down and took Dion's cock into her hand right as Zeph released it. Zeph bent lower across the god's big thigh and offered his ass to Theron, who swiftly took advantage. Dion gripped the West Wind by the back of the neck and devoured his mouth, his fingers still strumming Numa's clit.

Releasing Zephyrus with a low laugh, he gripped Numa by the hips. "No, little one. They will have the perfect vessel to drink from . . . your tasty snatch."

With that, he lifted her up. She reached out, flailing for

balance, and Cade and Zephyrus grasped each of her hands while Dion positioned her over his cock. The mere brush of his thick tip along the wet crease of her folds had her gasping, and she clutched at Cade's and Zeph's napes to tether herself through the rapture of the god's giant cock.

Dion slouched lower in his seat and pulled her back against him. Legs spread wide, she braced her feet on the edge of his seat on either side of his hips, using the leverage to raise herself up off his hips and back down to meet his upward thrust. He speared her hard with a deep grunt, then raised one arm to grasp a coiled vine dangling above his throne.

With a swift yank, the vine tore the barrier of heavy palm leaves away from the torrent of the waterfall behind Dion's throne, and a cascade of magic-rich water was diverted over his shoulders and down their joined bodies.

The cool wetness made Numa gasp and laugh, then moan in renewed pleasure when Zeph and Cade leaned in to tongue her water-slick breasts.

"We'll come as one to start, then it's all you, little one," Dion rumbled. The other four men clutched each other tighter. Bekim leaned over Cade's bent back and thrust harder into the big ursa. Dion had his hand between Cade's thighs, working his cock with quick, slapping strokes.

On Numa's other side, Theron rammed deep into Zephyrus, whose skin sparked with evidence of his ecstasy, sending pleasant tingles through his tongue where it teased her nipple. Dion firmly gripped Zeph's cock with his free hand, the West Wind's hips tilting rhythmically into the god's sure grip while Theron nailed him from behind.

Their auras were a wild clash of pleasure, and beyond the pavilion, the reveling partiers were tangled in their own wild orgies, though their gazes were all fixed on Dion's throne and the spectacle Numa was at the core of.

Her body was a tangled bundle of power, building up bit by bit with each thrust of Dion's cock and flick of her other lovers' tongues. She loved the convergence of all her mates' auras with its kaleidoscopic swirls of power mixing with hers. They rarely came together as a full group, preferring simpler combinations of two or three at a time, but today she would have them all. By the end of today's ritual, she would have a new life growing inside her, created from the combined essences of all five of these men she adored so much.

But until then, she had a task to complete—feeding as much power as possible to the center of the Haven, so Deva could make contact with the bloodline. It was not as onerous a task as the previous year's ritual to open a sky portal, but it was just as crucial to the safety of the higher races. And she intended to enjoy every second of it.

Dion groaned against her ear and released Cade's cock to hook her chin with one finger and pull her mouth to his. She latched on in a hungry kiss, her skin tingling with the crackle of their auras.

"Come for us, little one," Dion said.

"You first," she said, grinning at him and squeezing her core around his thick shaft. She used Cade and Zeph's shoulders for leverage to fuck Dion harder and the big god cursed, slamming up into her with a deafening bellow. His head flew back and water flooded down his chest, soaking the place where they were joined, but the cool liquid felt like nothing amid the heat of his orgasm.

The rush of divine power lit her entire body on fire, and her orgasm exploded from her as if she'd combusted from the inside. Her core clenched and bright heat washed through her. On either side of her, the four other men cursed and tensed, her Nirvana infusing them with pleasure as potent as what Dion had given her. Their orgasms lit them up like beacons and she clutched at Cade and Zephyrus, absorbing every last drop of magic they gave and focusing to let the Haven's water carry it where it needed to go.

Relaxing against Dion's torso, she hummed in contentment as the other men slowly extricated themselves from each other and slipped into one of the pools surrounding the throne.

"That was just the beginning, little one. Now it's time to share the wine."

He lifted her hips and slipped his erection out of her, then beckoned with one finger to the nearest group of a trio of nymphs who'd been tangled up with a pair of ursa males and a dragon. With hunger blazing in their eyes, they filed forward and fell to their knees between Dion's thighs. But it wasn't his cock they bowed for. Dion gripped Numa by her inner thighs and held her splayed wide as each of the supplicants dipped their heads and began to lick her clean of Dion's juices.

The revelers took turns, some bowing before her two at a time to drink the creamy offering Dion had spilled deep into her. Numa found herself in a near constant state of orgasmic bliss, thanks to the teasing rush of Dion's words in her ear and the brush of his fingers over her nipples.

Partway through, the crowd paused and waited long enough for Dion to bend her over in front of them and spear her from behind, filling her pussy with a fresh serving of the divine ambrosia that would fuel their fun for the rest of the day.

# CHAPTER 9

$\mathcal{D}$eva's eyes flew open and she let out a breathy "Oh!" when the first wave of power flooded from the water up through her body. Her skin tingled with a delightful combination of warmth and electricity. Across from her, Llyr's gaze was fixed on her face, intent and watchful despite his relaxed posture.

"How is it?" he asked.

Deva's nipples pricked and tingled, and she was acutely conscious of the tightness of her bodice around her chest, certain that if he looked, Llyr would be able to see clearly how aroused she was. But he only looked into her eyes, though his aura had brightened considerably.

"It's . . . amazing."

He dipped his head and in a rougher voice said, "That was god Nirvana . . . Part of it, anyway. And it will continue for some time—they're only just getting started. Why don't you test your link to the bloodline? See how far you can reach."

Deva nodded and closed her eyes, gripping the thick root she sat upon with both hands while she focused and reached out for the link.

In her mind, the bloodline blossomed, flowing outward from her consciousness like a web of brightly colored filaments. She tested the threads cautiously to gauge the strength of the links. They were strong, but only extended a short distance farther than the links she'd been aware of when first practicing the ritual.

"Not very far yet, but the links are strong. Dionysus said there were millions of humans who were part of the bloodline. Right now, all I can see are a few thousand. I think I need more power to reach farther. I don't want to waste energy on sending the message until I can get to all of them."

She opened her eyes and her heart skipped a beat at the hunger in Llyr's swirling aqua eyes. He blinked and looked away, then closed his eyes and nodded. "Done. The next group will join the ritual and add their power shortly. Remember to pace yourself. If you get overwhelmed, I'm here to help."

"You can feel it all too, can't you?" Deva asked, then added impulsively, "You'd be back there with the rest . . . participating . . . if you weren't with me, wouldn't you?"

Llyr exhaled slowly through his nostrils and nodded. "My brother Thiasoi are among the reveling nymphs in Dion's retinue. They are drunk on the god's ambrosia now. There is a strong chance they will find mates and perhaps even produce offspring today."

Deva's stomach clenched. "I'm sorry you got stuck with me."

His gaze returned to her, fierce and intense, and his jaw flexed. "I'm not sorry. And I'm not *stuck* with you, Deva.

"I have a confession to make. I lied yesterday. My brothers and I all volunteered to guard you when Neph made the request. When he revealed that only one of us could have the job, we nearly came to blows over who would have the honor. In the end, Neph made the choice because we were unable to compromise on our own.

"You were bound to us by blood inside that lab where Meri held us prisoner, but my brothers will break that link when they find nymphs to blood meld and build families with. I alone will keep that tie to you. Protecting you is my life now. I want nothing more than to fulfill that promise."

Deva took a shaky breath and shook her head. "But you're losing your chance to find a mate . . . to have a family. Neph could send any of the nymphs to take your place. You don't have to do this. They need you more than I do."

The briefest flash of hurt crossed his face and made her want to take back her words. She *did* need him if she intended to leave the higher realms and explore the human world, but it wasn't fair of her to. Not when his entire race needed him more. He and his Thiasoi brothers were the last males of their race who weren't spoken for. The other three would likely wind up with multiple nymphs apiece for mates in an effort to replenish the satyr numbers and strengthen the protection of the Haven. But Llyr would be trapped in a formal arrangement with her as her bodyguard.

"I made a vow to my leader. I won't break that."

A thought occurred to her that seemed both terrifying and exhilarating. "What if I chose you as my mate?"

Llyr went very still, his eyelids sliding closed as his aura flickered wildly. The conflicting signals made it difficult for Deva to understand what he was feeling. Was he angry at her for suggesting it?

"You shouldn't ask that," he finally said. "It isn't possible. Not when we still barely understand the full scope of your nature."

"It's because of my ursa side, isn't it?" She expelled an exasperated huff, irritated by his subtle reminder of how potentially dangerous her fertile magic could be, if she manifested the way most ursa females did.

"That, and the fact that your existence is completely beyond our grasp. You exist outside the normal flow of nymphaea magic. The River that allows us a glimpse into the current of time. We can't see any sign of what you will become, Deva. We have to be cautious."

A burning ache built in her belly. "What about what I *am* right now? I'm just a woman trying to understand who to be. I know I'm inexperienced, but I still have desires. I crave love. And a purpose. This ritual might be my only chance to prove myself, but I need more than this. I need someone to look at me and see more than just a mystery to solve. I'm a person too." Yet his comment about the lack of any sign of her path was a stark reminder of what was really wrong with her. She had no soul, so no wonder he refused her offer. How could she be his soul mate without that one crucial piece?

Her voice shook and her eyes burned, but another surge of the potent divine power flooded through her from the water at her feet, making her gasp in pleasure and sob at the same time. She clung to the tree root and clenched her eyes shut, struggling to hold back her tears.

When she opened her eyes, Llyr hovered in front of her, his dark brows tight with concern. He cupped her face with both hands and gazed into her eyes. "I see you, Deva. Trust me, I see you."

$\mathcal{A}$odh paced the length of the beachside bungalow Neph had led them to for their own part in the ritual. This was a corner of the Haven he'd rarely visited. When he and Neph had begun their affair so long ago, they'd meet in their secret temple garden beside the Nile rather than risk getting caught inside Neph's own realm. The secluded bungalow with the ocean view was far more comfortable, but despite the lulling crash of the surf, he couldn't shake the worry over enlisting Deva to help with the ritual, even though she had seemed more than eager to do so.

"It's time," Neph said, resting a hand on his shoulder.

Aodh turned and was instantly overwhelmed by the shared worry flooding the minds of both his mates. Their blood meld had grown stronger over the past year, and their emotions were particularly raw today. Vrishti slipped into his arms and pressed her face against his chest.

"She's frightened. I can feel it," Vrishti said. "But she's also determined to prove herself. She reminds me of myself when I decided to come find you last year." She turned her face up and met Aodh's gaze, then Neph's. "She can do this. I have faith in her."

But it wasn't just this ritual Aodh was worried about. "Are you sure Llyr was the right choice to guard her?" Aodh speared Neph with a challenging look. "I'm not sure I like the way he was looking at her when they left this morning."

"He knows not to cross the line," Neph said. "If he disobeys me, he'll be punished."

"What exactly *is* that line?" Aodh asked. "She's a highly sensitive girl. She craves validation . . . She already has an unhealthy attachment to Ozzie. Is there any reason to believe she won't transfer that need to Llyr?"

Neph gave him a helpless look. "What are we supposed to do? She's stagnating here, and we can't let her out into the human world without protection. Ozzie's no longer an option to watch her, and Llyr has the strongest link to her. If we want her powers to mature, we have to give her the freedom to explore them beyond the bounds of the Haven, or any of the other higher realms."

"Guys, can we give our daughter a little more credit? She's taking control of her life the best way she can, and I fully support letting *her* make those decisions for herself. Also, we probably ought to actually do the thing we really came here to do . . ." Vrishti reached up and placed a palm to Aodh's cheek, urging him to look down at her.

The Summer spirit blazed with fertile power behind Vrishti's eyes, and that spark was enough to dissolve Aodh's worry and ignite his desire. It helped that Vrishti's warm, sensual presence had seeped into his mind through their meld and was diverting his protective urges toward Deva into a more present, potent need.

"Perhaps you're right. She has three of the strongest females I know for mothers. Your influence will hopefully steer her well."

Vrishti gave him a sardonic look. "She will blossom if all her overbearing fathers give her the freedom to do so. If there is one thing I loved most about my own father, it was that he trusted me to decide what was best for myself. You can't dispute I made the right decisions, can you?"

Aodh chuckled at her subtle taunt. "I definitely have no room to object to your choices, Vrishti."

She pulled away from Aodh and stood between him and Neph, glancing between them. Coyly, she unfastened the toggle closure of the filmy robe she wore.

Neph's previously agonized expression smoothed as her gown fell partly open to reveal a stretch of brown skin and the luscious inner curves of her breasts. The very edges of the material were caught on both her erect nipples, still concealing them, but Aodh had a clear view of the center of her soft belly all the way down past her navel to the perfect black triangle of curls between her legs.

In one fluid motion, Neph moved behind her, his body morphing as he positioned himself at her back until he towered over Vrishti in his full primal satyr shape. He hooked one big hand around her jaw and tilted her head to the side, bending low to graze his lips along the curve of her neck. She looked so small, so delicate, in contrast to the huge, horned satyr, but Aodh was fully aware of how completely she owned both their primal beasts and could easily accommodate both dragon and satyr whenever she wished.

Her summer spirit blazed hot through her aura, her love and desire reflected in the intensity of the gaze she leveled on him. Neph's big fingers hooked the edge of her robe at her shoulders, but the satyr looked up at Aodh before proceeding.

"Are you just going to stand and watch?" Neph rumbled. "I am happy to fuck our mate for your entertainment."

Aodh's stiff cock twitched in his pants and he silently let

the conjured garment fade. Vrishti licked her lips, her gaze flitting down to his hips and back up. He closed the distance with a rough growl, framing her face in both hands and capturing her mouth with his. She moaned deliciously into the kiss, sliding her hands around his neck to tangle in the hair at his nape.

Behind her, Neph tugged her robe off her shoulders until it hung from her elbows. Her breasts grazed Aodh's bare chest, full and lush. He was constantly amazed at the potency of the hunger he always had for her, springing up hot and undeniable regardless of how sated she had left him the day before. Between them blazed the hot pulse of the dragon mark that graced the skin beneath her navel, directly over her womb. The brilliant glowing glyph was a reminder of Vrishti's near constant ache for them both to spill their seed into her and have it take root.

Mere days after the end of last year's war, she'd given them both the happy news that they would be fathers again. Though they both adored Deva, they weren't her only parents. Their new daughter, Neha, had become the singular focus of their lives since the very moment they sensed her tiny consciousness growing inside her mother.

Now Vrishti's body wanted another, and Aodh longed to give it to her, though he couldn't help but wonder whether Deva's uncommonly swift growth to adulthood had left an even greater need behind for Vrishti to nurture a child—or children—through their early years. He would give her as many babies as she wished for and would love them all every bit as much as he'd loved their first, even if Deva was never wholly theirs.

"How do you want us, kitten?" Neph rumbled at her back.

"We should be in the water," Vrishti murmured, and before Aodh could react, he sensed the pull of the drift. They landed in a splash only a few yards across the bungalow in the sunken stone pool on the deck that overlooked the sandy beach. A nearby stream fed the pool with refreshingly cool water that covered him to his waist, his feet solidly planted on the pebbled bottom.

Aodh laughed and pulled back to look at his mates. "We could have walked."

Vrishti giggled and grabbed his shoulders, hoisting herself up to reach eye-level with him. "We already wasted enough time today."

He cupped her bottom beneath the drenched fabric of her robe and hungrily accepted her kiss once more. She broke away breathlessly just long enough to allow Neph to finally divest her of the tangled, sodden garment. Then the satyr's hand found Aodh's cock and stroked it deftly, grazing the swollen tip along the hot seam of Vrishti's opening. Aodh and Vrishti both moaned into each other's mouths as Neph teased them with each other. The growing need made Aodh dizzy and he carefully stepped backward until his ass met the edge of the pool.

He sat on the smooth stone and shifted until the backs of his bent knees aligned with the very edge, his feet still dangling into the cool water. Breaking away from Vrishti, he lay down, his gaze still fixed on her face, his own adoration reflected in the deep summer green of her eyes. She crouched over him with her hands on his belly, her cheeks flushed, and her eyelids fluttering while Neph continued tormenting her slick clit and hot opening with the tip of Aodh's cock. Despite the torturous pleasure that shot through him with every squeeze and stroke, Aodh was far too enthralled by the transformation of Vrishti's pleasure from a relaxed, open-mouthed sigh, to more desperate clench of her brows accompanied by moans that betrayed her need to be fucked.

"Please," she begged, her fingernails digging into Aodh's

belly while she remained poised over his cock, seemingly paralyzed by Neph's almost casual hold on her hip.

"Lower, kitten," Neph said. She slipped her hands higher up Aodh's chest as she tilted toward him. "You want to feel him inside you?"

He squeezed Aodh's shaft, sending a spike of pleasure through his torso and eliciting a startled gasp of pleasure and a jerk of hips. Aodh desperately wanted to feel it, but the question hadn't been directed at him. He enjoyed this game they played, though, with Neph directing the fun, pretending Aodh's body was the prize if Vrishti followed all his commands.

"Yes," she sighed, her gaze fixed on Aodh's face. "I want his cock fucking me."

"Do you want to feel me inside you?" Neph asked in a gruffer tone.

"Oh, please, yes!" she said, shooting a desperate look over her shoulder.

"Where, kitten?" Neph's aqua eyes were a swirling maelstrom, his more severe satyr face the epitome of lust and carnal hunger. He gripped her shoulder and pushed her down until her chest flattened against Aodh's, leaving her round ass up in the air.

Impulsively, Aodh slid his hands down and grabbed both cheeks, squeezed them hard, then lifted his hands and smacked them. Vrishti squeaked in surprise and buried her face in Aodh's neck, teeth clamping down on his flesh.

"You like that?" he rumbled softly against her ear. She only responded with a shuddering moan and he glanced up to see Neph's face buried between her cheeks.

The satyr tongued her with abandon, still steadily stroking Aodh's cock and occasionally dipping his head and sliding his lips all the way down Aodh's thick shaft. He was going to go mad soon if he didn't get inside her, but he loved the way Neph seemed so intent on choreographing their pleasure before he took his own.

The satyr's aura betrayed his need, however, and Aodh was sure he would break very soon.

~

AS MUCH AS Vrishti ached to be fucked, she was too wound up in pleasure to tell Neph to stop. The satyr's tongue had captured all her breath, and it was all she could do just to cling to Aodh's big body to keep from losing her mind. When Neph slipped one finger into her ass, and then another, she understood he was on a mission.

Even though she'd recovered quickly after their daughter's birth, the added distraction of the baby had disrupted their normal routines. Neph's responsibilities leading the Haven beside his sister didn't help. This was the first time in months that the three of them had an entire day they could devote entirely to each other's pleasure.

Clearly, Neph was determined to waste no time. Her ass tingled with pleasure and pain in equal measure when he slid a third digit into her. She trembled with need for more, her abandoned core hot and aching.

When she let out a harsh plea, Aodh grabbed the sides of her head and urged her to look at him. His pale eyes blazed. "I hope you're ready to get good and fucked today, baby. Your ass is about to get a workout."

The big satyr shifted positions, and in her periphery she caught sight of him tilting a clay bottle over her back as he lifted one wet, hooved foot out of the water to brace on the edge of the pool.

Cool oil drizzled out of the bottle, around the three fingers he had buried in her ass, and up her spine. The liquid trickled down her sides and Aodh slicked his hands through it, spreading it farther down her sides and back up to coat her heavy breasts with it. He toyed with her nipples, sending tingling heat back to her aching core and lifted his hips until the head of his cock pressed against her entrance.

"Please fuck me," she whimpered.

"In a second," he rumbled in her ear. "He's almost there."

Gaia's tears, he had her ass so full already she was afraid she'd come to pieces if he did any more. Neph's hot, heavy shaft grazed her ass cheek as he moved into position, his body casting a shadow over her back.

Vrishti closed her eyes when the length of Neph's thick erection stroked once along the place where his fingers plunged into her. Then his fingers disappeared, only to be replaced by the hot, round, bulbous head of his cock.

She held her breath when he speared her stretched opening, then let it out in a loud cry as Aodh lifted his hips in a sudden jerk, instantly filling her pussy from beneath. Before she could even process the fullness of their invasion, her orgasm tore through her, but she was at their mercy and unable to do anything but surrender to their cocks both fucking her.

She clung to Aodh for dear life to weather the pleasure, more intense than any she'd felt since the first day she'd been blessed to have them both at once. Behind her Neph let out a resonant roar and pulled his cock free of her ass. The sound of slick smacking still continued behind her and she shot a fevered look over her shoulder to see him intently stroking his immense cock until thick white ribbons of semen erupted from his tip, the hot fluid landing squarely at the sensitive opening he'd just vacated.

Beneath her, Aodh stiffened, his cock swelling in her tight channel, then flooding her with his own hot seed. He squeezed her ass hard as he pumped up into her a few more times, then fell still. But he only paused for a breath before he had her up and off him and flipped her around, her back flush against his chest.

"My turn in that tight ass," he rumbled. He hooked his arms beneath her knees and sat up, cradling her against his chest with her legs spread wide. Vrishti grabbed at his arms to hold on, still tingling and dazed from the body-warping orgasm their first round of fucking had inflicted on her.

"Relax, baby," Aodh murmured against her ear as he lowered her onto his cock. She closed her eyes and bit her lip, waiting for the pain of yet another immense cock burying itself in her tender backside, but his passage was eased by the hot remnants of Neph's orgasm coating her opening.

Her eyes fluttered open as Aodh teased her clit while he pumped up into her. Before her, Neph had sunk low into the water but now rose, sluicing suds off his cock and rinsing it clean. He stalked toward her and fell to his knees between her thighs. His big horns came as high as her shoulders when he buried his face against her soaked folds.

She grabbed on, letting her head fall back against Aodh's shoulder while they carried her through another orgasm, Aodh's cock thrusting rhythmically into her ass while Neph sucked hungrily at her clit.

No sooner had that orgasm faded than Neph straightened and plunged his cock into her in one single, urgent thrust. The pair of them proceeded to fuck her until her ass and pussy both were flooded with their spend once more.

With limp limbs, Vrishti succumbed to Neph's gentle tug and fell into his arms, sighing. He'd shrunk to his human size once more and carried her to the center of the pool, chuckling softly while he held her. "That was only the beginning, kitten. We'll be at this all day until we get word that Deva's completed the ritual and transmitted the message. Judging from Llyr's account of the progress, she'll need all of us sending constant power to her before there's enough."

"I can handle it," she said, giving him a goofy, lust-drugged smile.

Aodh slipped up to her other side, and the pair of them supported her head while she floated on the surface of the water. They gazed down at her adoringly. "We have no doubt," he said. "We can take it slow for the rest of the day, though."

Vrishti sighed and stared up into the lush foliage above their pool. Both men had dipped their heads to lap at each of her breasts, their sucking easing the ache of mother's milk that had built up since she'd said goodbye to their daughter early the day before. As they suckled her, their free hands traced random patterns down her belly and between her thighs. Then their fingers found her core again and she spread herself open for them. She moaned under their gentle ministrations that swiftly turned to more determined strokes. They brought her swiftly to another orgasm with only their hands, then Neph moved down and positioned himself between her thighs and pushed in deep.

"Let me have you both together," she said, shooting a pleading look up at Aodh who still hovered near her head, one arm hooked under her shoulders to support her where she floated.

He bent to kiss her. "Anything you wish."

She reached out and Neph took her hands, pulling her up into his embrace while Aodh moved into position at her back. Together they lifted her just high enough to allow them to come together at the hips. When she slipped back down, sandwiched close between their strong bodies, both their long, hard cocks speared her core.

This was the fullness she preferred. To be filled to the brim with the pair of them on either side, moving as one being in search of her pleasure. She gazed deep into Neph's hypnotic eyes, his look pulling her consciousness into that whirlpool that led straight to his soul. Within those depths, she lost herself to them both, as sure as she ever was that together they could accomplish anything.

# CHAPTER 11

"Oh Gaia," Deva breathed, startled by the overwhelming sense of love that flooded into her with the newest surge of magic. Tears sprang to her eyes when she understood what that meant. The mating bond between her ursa mother and her mates was so strong it left Deva craving the kind of connection they had.

"What is it?" Llyr asked.

"So beautiful . . . their love. Have you ever felt anything like that?"

Llyr's jaw clenched and he swallowed before shaking his head. "My duty comes first." After a second, his features softened and he smiled. "But I am happy for Neph. All the Thiasoi believed he'd foregone mating in solidarity with us, but then Nyx mated Nereus and the precedent of the Thiasoi staying unmated was broken. Then we thought he and Meri might . . ." He shook his head and snorted in disgust.

"He nearly mated her," Deva said. "I'm glad he didn't, even if it turned out badly. It means I'm here."

"Yes," Llyr said, reaching out and wrapping his hands

around both her ankles beneath the water. The charge of arousal from his touch was disorienting. He laughed ruefully. "I could have done without the torture, but I'm glad you're here too." He slipped his hands up to her calves and gave them a squeeze. "How does the power level feel? What can you sense?"

Deva blinked at him, distracted by the warmth of his hands and the tingle of pleasure that coursed through her even stronger than the steady buzz she'd felt from the power she'd absorbed. But he was talking about the bloodline, not his touch. Forcing herself to refocus, she closed her eyes and reached for the bloodline again. The number of threads had quadrupled, but was still not expansive enough to account for all of them.

"Tell them I need more still."

"Will do."

She opened her eyes and watched his face as his eyelids fell shut. He possessed the same angular features and upturned, half-moon eyes as many of the nymphs, though with him and his Thiasoi brothers it was more pronounced. His hair was shiny, silken cascade, falling in blue-black waves around his broad, tan shoulders.

Deva liked the way his fairer skin tone stood out against her deep brown shade where his hands held her lower legs. His fingers seemed to involuntarily flex, squeezing, then loosening, but never completely releasing her.

Sitting there watching him, she was struck by the urge to sing. She started humming softly, closing her eyes and composing a tune in her head while she waited for more power from the ritual. When a slow, rhythmic tapping picked up against her calf in time with her humming, she opened her eyes and smiled.

"That was beautiful," Llyr said.

She lifted a shoulder. "It was for you."

His brow twitched. "I am honored, though I doubt I am anywhere near special enough to have earned a song."

"That's up to me, isn't it? You're my protector." She thought about Ozzie and the place he held in her heart. A small part of her quaked with guilt over allowing this feeling to blossom for someone else, but she'd grown up around women who all had an abundance of love to share with multiple mates, and no one seemed to want for more. Her aunt Numa's five mates all adored her, and she remembered the day Numa had made the choice to love all of them. Deva envied all the other women their freedom and the adoration of their men, and their brilliant, powerful souls they had to bind to their lovers'.

"I am, and I didn't make that vow lightly. Even though I am here by Neph's command, I am yours until you choose to release me from my promise."

"What if I want to keep you forever?"

His mouth quirked. "Then you should save your breath, because I'm capable of far more song-worthy acts than sitting around in a puddle with you."

Deva's hungry mind refocused, reminded that Llyr was her key to exploring the human world. "Do you know a lot about humans? About their world?"

He shifted toward her and slipped his hands up to cup the backs of her knees, tapping his thumbs on her kneecaps. "Not much yet. I was out of touch for so long, trapped in Meri's lab. But my brothers and I spent the past year getting reacquainted with the world." He tilted his head as though considering. "Humanity is different than it used to be. But still the same, in a lot of ways. There is a lot to see—to experience." Then he grinned. "The music is amazing."

"Did you see a lot of our kind while you were there? Did you see any turul?" She was a tangle of questions, but forced herself to bite her tongue. She wanted to *experience* it all more than she wanted to hear him talk about it. But there was one thing she desperately wanted to know and was afraid to ask.

Llyr's eyes narrowed and he shot her a knowing smile that made heat creep up her neck. "I spent some time with your father—Nikhil—and his mates and their band. They call themselves 'Fate's Fools,' which is depressingly appropriate." He chuckled and shook his head, then met her gaze again, watchful. "Ozzie West was there. He asked about you."

The heat in her cheeks turned molten. Not even the truth of the ritual she was part of had fazed her, but the mere mention of Ozzie had her flustered to a shameful degree. "What did he say?"

"Nothing specific. Just asked if you were well. It was odd, though, because he had your father *right there*, yet he pulled me aside to ask. You'd visited Neph just the week before, so I'd seen you but only from afar. I told him that as far as I knew, you were great. That was pretty much the extent of it. I think he was a little drunk."

Deva chewed on her lower lip, aching to ask more, but unwilling to admit the depth of her longing to know what kept Ozzie away.

Llyr lifted a hand and pressed his thumb to her chin, forcing her to release her lip from her teeth. "What worries you so much? Do you miss him?"

"Yes. But it's been so long since I've seen him. I'm afraid he's forgotten me. He didn't come to the Haven for Equinox, either."

"Do you blame him? He's a turul without a mate, and he already knows everyone who would be here. If any of us were his *One*, he'd have known already. I think if I knew for certain my mate wasn't in the Haven, I'd avoid the place too, especially on a day like today."

A lump formed in her throat, blocking the words of

denial she felt surge up. Ever since she'd returned from the safety of the god realm, she'd had the strongest sense of *belonging* whenever she looked at Ozzie. The last time she'd seen him, she could have sworn she felt a bond, but that had been ages ago. It was like he was avoiding her, and it hurt like hell to believe he didn't want to see her. To hear that he'd asked about her . . . Gaia, she was so confused.

Tears burned at the corners of her eyes and she clamped her teeth down on her lower lip again in a struggle to keep from crying.

"Deva, what is it?" Llyr asked.

She shook her head and pulled away when he rested his hand on her cheek. She hated that he was here to witness her confusion, her weakness over what was likely a complete misunderstanding owing to the fact that she was too young and inexperienced with love to know any better. But the nauseating burn in her belly felt real.

"Deva, look at me." Llyr's stern tone snapped her attention to him. Concern darkened his eyes, his brows curling inward. Gently, he said, "Talk to me."

She gave a little shake of her head. "I . . . can't."

He slipped his hand to the side of her neck, his thumb idly grazing the line of her jaw. She wished he would either stop looking at her or say something . . . redirect the conversation to anything but Ozzie . . . but his gaze kept flicking between her mouth and her eyes. Finally, his eyes slowly closed and he licked his lips, and she was sure that was the end of it. But when his eyes opened again, they were filled with a crazed determination.

His tightened his grip on her neck, and before she could take a breath, he leaned forward and pressed his mouth to hers. At the same instant, an overwhelming surge of power flowed up her legs from the water and she grabbed hold of Llyr's shoulders in a desperate attempt to cling to sanity.

But her embrace only encouraged him. He emitted a deep groan and wrapped his arms around her, pulling her down onto his lap and tight against his big, hard body. Deva surrendered to his kiss, hyperaware of every place their bodies came into contact, but oblivious of the water soaking her gown once again. She was blissfully grateful that Llyr had chosen this as the way to make her forget her confusion over Ozzie.

# CHAPTER 12

"*D*o you hear singing?" Assana asked.

Gavra nuzzled the back of her ear, then tugged the strap of her wispy gown off her shoulder, following his fingers with his lips. "Thought that was in my head," he said, peeling the fabric off her breast and letting it fall. Silas dipped his head and captured Assana's bared nipple and she sighed, pushing her soft, round backside into Gavra's erection. She raked her fingers through Silas's hair, pulling his sucking mouth closer as though he were a babe and not a full-grown man about to fuck her.

"I didn't think any turul were here besides your brother's and sister's mates," she murmured. "It doesn't sound like a male voice, though. Is that Evie?"

Gavra closed his eyes to listen, still making quick work of Assana's dress. He pushed the spare fabric over her hips and it fell to the ground in a hiss. Then he gripped her ass and squeezed, sliding his cock along the cleft between her cheeks and reveling in the friction against his heated flesh.

The song filtered through the air as clear as a bell, but his desire was too strong to care what it signified or who sang it.

Silas rose up in front of Assana and clasped her head in both hands, covering her mouth in a ravenous kiss. Through their meld, Gavra sensed his ursa mate's desperate desire and the encroaching discomfort of his pheronesis rising once more. Perfect timing for the man to be afflicted with the common condition all male ursa dealt with every few months of their lives when they were young. Silas was only in his twenties, and this was the third time he'd been through it since their mating the year before. Gavra and Assana were more than happy to accommodate his needs.

"Come," Assana said, grabbing both their hands and leading them the few steps to the crystal-clear pool just outside the door of her private bungalow. A small waterfall cascaded over the wet rock wall above, filling the secluded area with pale mist. Dew condensed on Assana's skin, making her look like she was coated in diamonds as she stepped naked into the pool and swam to a rock near the waterfall. She climbed up and turned around to wait for them, water sliding off her naked body.

Silas plunged in, reaching her with only a few quick strokes and emerging from the water directly between her spread thighs. She reclined partway on one elbow and dipped her other hand between her legs, opening herself for the ursa.

"You don't have to wait, Silas. I know you're hurting."

Silas dropped his hand to grip his cock, but he shook his head. "I need to taste you first. Your flavor is as much of a painkiller as being buried inside you."

He hooked his arms beneath her thighs and hauled her to the very edge of the rock, then buried his face between her legs. Assana's mouth opened and her head fell back, though her gaze remained locked on Gavra's. He lingered at the edge of the pool for a few moments longer, content to watch his mates, entranced by the perfect harmony of their auras as their mutual need increased.

When Assana was close to breaking, he stepped into the water and waded across to them, stopping only when he reached Silas's back. The other man moaned against Assana's wet folds when Gavra slipped a hand around his hips and gripped Silas's stiff, throbbing length and began to stroke.

"You can have us both this time," Gavra rumbled into the ursa's ear, gratified by the shiver of pleasure that coursed through Silas's body when Gavra pressed his own aching hard-on against his ass beneath the water. "Do you want me inside you while you fuck her? Or do you want me to give you my ass for a change?"

A low growl rumbled up from deep in Silas's chest and Assana let out a throaty laugh. "I think you found a winner. But which is it?"

Silas pulled away from Assana's juicy petals, his chest heaving. "I want to fuck you both until I can't feel my goddamn dick anymore."

Gavra expelled a surprised laugh, his mirth mirrored by Assana's delighted smile. He subsided to a low chuckle, pressing his forehead to Silas's shoulder, then groaned when Silas reached back and gave his cock a squeeze. The ursa's touch turned into a more urgent stroke and Gavra bit down on his shoulder.

"You haven't offered in a while," Silas said. "I'm damn sure not going to pass up this chance."

"Looking forward to it," Gavra said. "But as soon as you're done, your ass is mine."

"It always was," Silas said, turning to face him and yanking him into a fevered kiss.

Gavra responded with equal fervor, relishing his lover's swelling aura and the spark of pleasure that shot through him when their cocks brushed together. A cool, light stroke grazed his jaw and shoulder, followed by another pair of lips, and he broke away from Silas to wrap his arm around Assana and bend to kiss her.

Even in this loose embrace with the two of them, Gavra's need soared. The intensity of his love for these two made his very bones ache to see them satisfied in whatever way pleased them most, and he sensed that need reflected in their bond.

"It's all about you today, Silas," Assana said. Her hand dropped down between them, knuckles grazing Gavra's cock as she took Silas into her hand and stroked. The ursa's entire body shuddered under Assana's touch, and Gavra stepped back as Silas turned to her. With a primal growl, Silas hooked his arms beneath Assana's ass and set her back down on the rock, dipping his head to her breasts as he positioned himself between her thighs.

Assana's attention was wholly fixed on Silas, but their bond betrayed her awareness of Gavra and she silently called, beckoning inside her mind for him to come to her and not just stand and watch. He climbed up onto the rock and reclined beside her just in time to see Silas's cock slide home into her waiting depths in a single, quick thrust. Gavra's entire body buzzed from the transfer of sensation through their meld, Assana's rough moan of pleasure reverberating down his spine as though he were the one being fucked and not her.

"It will be you soon enough," Silas said, turning his dark gaze to Gavra as he pulled back and thrust deep again. Assana's head fell back and she slid her long legs up Silas's sides.

Gavra scooted closer until his stiff cock brushed Assana's hip. He dipped his head to capture her nipple in his mouth, opening his mind as wide as possible to absorb every single sensation that passed through his lovers' bodies.

They hadn't always been so free with each other over the past year. For the first few months, it was all they could do to tear themselves away from each other. He'd experienced Assana's pregnancy with a mind more open than he'd ever had with any of his past human mates, and his love for both his mates had bloomed. But he'd also experienced their darker moments with as much clarity.

First Silas's pheronesis and the pain that accompanied it, and then Assana's labor, which had been as terrifying as it was beautiful. The feedback nearly destroyed them in the midst of the hardest parts of Assana's pregnancy and their son's birth. Through those experiences, they came to the realization that it exhausted them all too much to remain so deep within each other's souls during the darker times. They concluded that they should maintain their boundaries as much as possible, so if one of them were weak, the other two would not be brought low in the process and could combine their strength to make up the difference and help the other through.

Now the only time they opened themselves so completely was when they made love, and it was all the sweeter for the distance they kept in between.

"Need more," Silas growled. He pushed Assana's thighs wider and bent over, capturing her other nipple in his mouth. She arched into them both, driving her fingers through Gavra's hair as he laved her breast with his tongue.

He released her nipple and turned his head, gazing in rapt fascination at the place where she and Silas were joined. She released his head, and a moment later wrapped her hand around his cock and began to stroke.

Silas groaned in pleasure, his hips picking up tempo as they smacked against Assana's thighs. Their bodies glistened with the dewy spray from the waterfall, the late morning sun filtering through the mist casting them in an ethereal glow.

The moment felt a little surreal as inundated with pure pleasure as it was. Assana tightened her grip around his cock, her strokes quickening as their auras swelled. Gavra slipped his hand down her belly to find her swollen clit hot and slick with her juices.

Assana and Silas both cried out harsh affirmations when Gavra began to toy with her tight bud. Silas reared back, grabbing Assana by the backs of her knees and staring down between them as though he needed to see the pleasure taking place to believe it.

"Fuck, that's good," he blurted. "I missed this so fucking much."

Gavra chuckled and pushed himself up onto one arm, careful not to dislodge Assana's hand from his cock. He bent down with his head at Assana's navel, his gaze fixed on the tight stretch of Silas's cock filling her gorgeous snatch. With his free hand, he held her folds apart and dipped his head lower, stretched out his dragon tongue, and tickled her sensitive flesh with its tip.

"Oh, fuck yes," Silas said, his words nearly drowned out by the harsh cry erupting from Assana's lips. "Make her come on my cock."

Assana's hand disappeared from Gavra's shaft, and a second later, she dug her fingernails into his neck. Her hips bucked up into Silas, her belly slick under Gavra's cheek as he lapped at her clit with deliberate circular strokes.

She arched her back and yelled out an incoherent plea. All at once, Gavra's mind blasted with her intense pleasure, her body torqueing beneath his cheek and both her hands clutching at his head and shoulders as she fell apart. Sweet nectar flooded his tongue from her climax, complementing the delicious rush of magic that spilled through his skin.

Silas abruptly pulled out and smacked Gavra on the ass. "Need your ass *now*."

Dizzy from the rush Assana's Nirvana had given him, he drunkenly complied, twisting around to face Assana again and swinging his leg across her hips. Behind him, Silas still stroked himself with fevered speed.

With his free hand, he gripped one of Gavra's cheeks, spreading him open and teasing his thumb around Gavra's opening. Gavra buried his face against Assana's shoulder, both anxious and eager for what was to come.

Silas was right—he didn't offer his ass up to his lovers often, preferring to be the one who orchestrated their pleasure and watching as often as he participated. But he loved this more for how rarely it happened, and especially for how enthusiastically they both tended to his needs when he gave into them.

Assana clutched his head, forcing him to turn and face her. He peered into the swirling aqua depths of her gaze and lost himself to the sensations—her lips captured his at the same moment her hand reached between them and began to stroke him again. And behind him, Silas emitted a harsh curse, his semen spattering hot and thick against Gavra's exposed opening. Another surge of potent power flooded Gavra's body and he groaned, barely able to hold it together.

Silas stroked his thumb harder around Gavra's opening, spreading his seed and teasing the tip of his thumb gently in and out past the slick, tight barrier. Jolts of sensation shot through Gavra. He could easily come right now just from their attention, but with their power combined with his own when he finally found his peak, he'd be able to send a more powerful dose to the Source.

Until then, he'd savor every rising wave of pleasure.

"Fuck, do you have any idea how much I love it when you give yourself to us like this?" Silas said, his voice rough. He continued teasing Gavra's ass, now with both hands grasping his cheeks, spreading him wide. His thumbs caressed the sensitive, puckered flesh and pushed in and out in a maddening rhythm.

"You mean when I let you torture me?" Gavra retorted.

Assana laughed, her breasts pushing up into Gavra's chest with delightful pressure and warmth. "You love it. Now why don't you get inside me?"

She shimmied beneath him until she could get her legs out from under him and slung around his waist, then lifted her hips up off the rock, grazing her soft, slick core along his length. His cock ached to feel her tight sheath, but Silas had him trapped and the exquisite pleasure being inflicted on him from behind was too good for him to move.

"Need a little help if you want that," he rumbled, peering down at Assana's glistening cheeks. His thundering heartbeat crescendoed at the sight of the watery beauty beneath him, her primal essence bleeding through her human form. Her skin had taken on a blue-green sheen, her lips a pearlescent blue. A nearly manic need flooded her gaze as though she hadn't just climaxed.

She wrapped one arm around his shoulders and tightened her thighs around his hips, easily leveraging herself up until she could position his tip at her entrance. Her eyelids fluttered closed and her head fell back as she shifted her body down his just enough to take him into her. The tight, hot friction flooded him with unbearable pleasure and he hooked an arm around her back, pulling her tighter to him as she began to move, writhing and twisting to pump her hips up and down along his engorged length.

He struggled to keep his hips still, unwilling to break contact with Silas's touch. The stretching push of thumbs in his ass disappeared and was swiftly replaced by the hot, thick tip of his cock.

Through their meld, they both knew the exact moment to move. Assana suddenly tightened her grip with arms and legs around him, her deliciously tight pussy clamping down on his cock at the same second Silas shoved home. Gavra let out a strangled roar and reared back, taking Silas even deeper as the ursa grabbed his hips and braced his knees on either side.

Silas sank his teeth into Gavra's shoulder and groaned, beginning to steadily pump up into his ass with slow, agonizingly perfect thrusts. It took nearly all Gavra's strength to maintain his hold on Assana and let them both dictate the movements. He was pinned between them, the gorgeous, sex-crazed nymph fucking herself on his cock in front and the hormone-drunk ursa buried in him from behind.

He reached back and clutched at Silas's hip with one hand urging him on, then captured Assana's mouth and simply let himself go. His mind and body opened to the pleasure completely, his soul awash with every fresh impression of their love and desire. He soaked it all in, letting it fill him to bursting and then some, until finally he found his limit.

Assana cried out his name and Silas echoed the call as the pair of them flooded him with their orgasms, inundating him with fresh, potent magic. At the same second, he let loose all the power he'd held in check, his cock spasming and filling Assana's sweet, hot depths while he diverted the magic he'd stored up into the misty air and water that surrounded them, sending it to the center of the Haven and their last hope to keep their world whole.

GAVRA COLLAPSED in a tangle of his lovers' limbs, one foot dangling off the rock into the cool water. He kept his eyes closed, focusing on the flow of magic seeping out of him into the pool through very little effort on his part. That the Haven's own waters were so connected had never occurred to him, but it stood to reason. If all the earth's waters could give access to the Haven, why shouldn't all the Haven's waters link to the Source itself?

A lovely, lilting sound filled the air around him and he tilted his head to listen.

"You hear it, don't you?" Assana whispered.

"Mm . . . it sounds like a turul mating song . . ."

He trailed off, brows creasing. There were a handful of female turul in the Haven today, but they were all happily mated. He listened harder, trying to decide if he was mishearing and it was a male voice. Perhaps Ozzie had decided to join in the ritual after all and was hoping to lure a nymph. But that made no sense. Ozzie had spent enough time in the Haven over the past year to know unequivocally whether his One were among the nymphs. If he were certain enough to stay away, that meant she wasn't here.

And that voice was most definitely female. In fact, it sounded like his niece, who had a voice as beautiful as Evie's.

"It's Deva," he said, finally opening his eyes. Silas paused while cleaning himself and frowned. He and Assana exchanged a quick look before they both turned to Gavra, identical thoughts at the forefront of their minds a split-second before Assana spoke them out loud.

"Should we be worried? She's so young."

"She wasn't too young for Dion to enlist her help," Silas said.

Within his lover's mind, Gavra caught a glimpse of Deva as she'd appeared that morning, radiant and eager to begin. She'd been beautiful, and seen through the filter of the young ursa's gaze, every bit the sensual woman who *should* be at the core of a ritual like the one they were undertaking today.

Gavra didn't see her that way. To him she was a child, despite her unusual origin and speedy growth to woman-hood. He narrowed his gaze at Silas, who gave him a sheepish look.

"I can't help how I see her," Silas said. "And you can't deny she craves a purpose as much as I did when you met me. You've seen how fucking brilliant her aura is with that drive . . . that hunger to learn. Why shouldn't she want to learn about love too? If there's anything I learned last year, it's that *none* of us could have fulfilled our purpose without our mates. I would not be the man I am today without the two of you."

"You think she wants a mate?" Assana asked, darting a look between Gavra and Silas.

"She's far too young yet for a mate," Gavra growled.

Silas gave him an incredulous look. "I beg to differ. Dragons may start late, but ursa and nymphaea become sexually mature in our twenties or earlier. If that's a turul song, maybe her turul side is the one maturing now. How early do they start?"

Gavra's jaw ticked. This did not bode well.

"Well?" Silas asked, crossing his arms over his broad chest, water droplets trickling down his belly.

"Turul can recognize their soul mates in childhood—it has happened. But it's impossible for her to have one."

"I don't see how . . ."

"She has no soul, Silas," he snapped. "Therefore, she can't have a soul mate."

Silas's mouth dropped open and he nodded slowly. "Right . . ." He snorted. "Then no wonder she's trying so damn hard to find one."

# CHAPTER 13

Deva let the song fade into the misty air and took a slow breath, her heart pounding. Llyr's fingers tightened at her hips and she dropped her gaze back down to his face, bracing herself. It was silly for her to break into song in response to a kiss, but it had been a special kiss to her.

Her first kiss.

She was acutely aware of how close they were. He'd pulled her onto his lap and now they sat half-submerged in the water, her knees bracketing his hips and his thighs beneath her butt. Her hands rested on his forearms, still gently tapping the rhythm of the song that had faded a moment ago.

She swallowed and forced herself to still her fingers and to school her expression to indifference, but was sure she failed.

Llyr's eyes were a hypnotic swirl she wished she could interpret, and she hoped the fierce grip he had on her hips was a *good* thing and not something to worry about.

She bit her lip and blinked, suddenly overwhelmed by the

belief that she'd disappointed him somehow, and when he tore his gaze away and fixed his eyes on some distant point, her heart lurched.

"Why did you sing that?" he choked.

"I—I couldn't help it. Sometimes singing is like a stress response, I guess. Did you not like it?"

His big chest rose and fell with a deep sigh and he returned his gaze to her. Deva clutched at his arms, grateful for the continued contact that grounded her despite the uncertainty of what he might say next.

"I loved it, but I don't deserve it. I am not the man for you, Deva. I'm only your guardian. Besides, isn't there something between you Ozzie West?"

Deva pressed her lips together, but relaxed her grip on his arms, running her hands up and over his biceps and back down as she considered how to respond. The contact on its own felt good, and she liked how he looked at her even though his aura was wild with conflicting emotions. *He* liked the contact too, which was apparent to her on many fronts. Despite his wavering aura, he hadn't stopped holding her and his eyes kept drifting back to her mouth, his aura spiking bright red-gold each time.

Not to mention his sarong did little to conceal his arousal, even under the water.

"You know I am part ursa, right?" she said. "And ursa females choose their mates. And they rarely choose only a single male. I don't see why I can't choose you both if I want."

Llyr's hands shifted toward her low back as if he wanted her closer, though his words were a contradiction. "I am not saying you can't have more than one. Just that one of them shouldn't be *me*. I am here to serve you however you need, but I made a vow to Neph that I would not indulge myself with you. Your nature . . . well, it's *because* you are part ursa, really. Do you even know what that song signified? What you were really asking for?"

"Love?" she asked.

"No, Deva. Not just love. I have heard turul mating songs before, and the one thing they all have in common is a promise to bind one's soul to another. To do that requires the two people to join their bodies. To make love so deeply their souls meet. Your song was a promise to me, and I can't accept that promise because I made a promise to your father that precludes it. I will guard you and help you through this ritual however you need, but that's where my role must end."

She narrowed her eyes at him, at the lack of conviction in his voice combined with the comfortable, familiar way his thumbs drifted back and forth over her sides through the waterlogged fabric of her dress.

"Then why did you kiss me?"

Llyr chuckled and shrugged. "You looked lost, and I needed you to stay focused on the moment. Ozzie isn't here. I can tell that bothers you. If kissing you keeps you grounded, I'd do it again. In fact, I will do anything short of actually fucking you, as long as you keep things in perspective."

"Why not that? What if fucking is what I need to keep things in perspective?" She was grateful for the cool water surrounding her lower body; she might have overheated otherwise.

"Because we don't know how much of your ursa nature is tied to your fertility. Short of waiting for you to hit estrous, we have no way to tell."

Her brows lifted as she realized what he meant. How much did he really know? "But you aren't an ursa . . . I thought it was pregnancy that was the risk. If you can't get me pregnant, why worry?"

He lifted a shoulder and let it drop. "We don't know I

can't. My link to you is like a blood meld, so we have to assume it works the same as one where pregnancy is concerned. You're a complete mystery to us. All we know for certain is that you *can* reach all those humans out there if we feed you enough power." His brow twitched and he dipped his head. "Speaking of which . . . get ready for another surge."

Deva nodded and closed her eyes, focusing on her link to the bloodline. The entire lower half of her body began to tingle a moment later, and she gasped when a wave of raw power rushed through her lower limbs even more swiftly than before. Her muscles tensed and relaxed, leaving her pleasantly euphoric as even more of the bloodline emerged, a web of brilliant little lights that filled her mind.

"I need to be deeper, I think," she said, keeping her eyes shut and focusing on the unyielding low-frequency hum of magic that seemed to be part of the water now. "Support me under the water."

"Whatever you need," Llyr said, sliding his hands up her back and shifting his body forward to hold her suspended just beneath the surface as she lay back. "Put your legs around my waist. I've got you."

She let him guide her until her entire body save her face was submerged. She stretched her calves around his hips, which forced him closer between her thighs, and hooked her ankles together at his low back. The change in position provided a more complete connection with the water and the current of magic.

"How is that?" Llyr asked, his voice a low rumble partly muffled by the water that lapped over her ears.

"Better, but I still don't have enough for a complete connection. We're halfway there, though. I think . . ." She bit her lip, hesitating to admit something that had occurred to her as the water seeped through her gown. The fabric was completely saturated, but she could still feel a void in magic where it covered her skin. She felt ridiculous for freaking out over it earlier.

"I meant it when I said I'm here for you, Deva," Llyr said. "Tell me what you need and I'll do it."

"I don't need you to do anything." She kept her eyes shut to maintain the courage to tell him. "But I think I need to be naked."

Before she could chicken out, she mentally dissolved the conjured gown. At her back, Llyr's hands warmed now that there was no dress separating his skin from hers. He remained dead silent and statue-still, and Deva slowly opened her eyes, uncertain what she would see.

Llyr's eyes were a maelstrom of whirling energy, his aura a vivid red. She couldn't see his hips from this angle, but didn't need to. The hard ridge of flesh pressed between her thighs was a searing reminder of how she affected him.

"Are you all right?" she asked. Her voice seemed to snap him out of some sort of trance and his eyes cleared to a vibrant, placid aqua. He smiled.

"Never better," he said and lifted his brows. "Decided the dress was overrated, did you? After all that fuss earlier."

The teasing tone made her smile wider and she used her hold on his hips to leverage herself into a sitting position. "I never realized how much easier it is to absorb the magic through my skin."

"Dragon skin is like that," Llyr said. "Especially the erogenous zones. A dragon's horns and his cock absorb power even more easily than his hands."

"How do you know so much about all the other races?"

"Thiasoi training when I was young. We were forbidden from mating between the races before, but not from enjoying sex with each other. We had to understand where the limits were so we could avoid crossing the line."

"So you also know that you can't impregnate a dragon

unless she's marked you and wants to bear your child." She had also been educated in all the races' various differences, but only in an effort to become better acquainted with her own nature.

He gave her a quizzical look. "True . . . What are you suggesting?"

"Nothing at all. Just making sure we understand each other." She gave him a sweet smile and leaned in to kiss him, enjoying the warmth of his body now that there was no barrier between them, save the waterlogged sarong around his hips.

Llyr's hands slid up her back and he eagerly returned the kiss, his enthusiasm still at odds with his cautious language earlier. But one thing she had learned about the nymphaea was that they were by nature a hedonistic race, so it should come as no surprise that he would happily indulge in the pleasure of a simple, harmless kiss. As long as she kept things in *perspective*.

When they broke away, she had the urge to sing again, but stifled it and sighed instead.

"What is it?" he asked, so acutely attuned to her moods through their blood meld. She had liked that quality at first, but regretted it now. She didn't want to give him another reason to dismiss her growing affection for him.

"This feels nice," she said, slipping her arms around his shoulders and laying her cheek against his chest. Her legs hooked over a big, smooth root that created a ledge past which the Source's waters cascaded to another pool below. The water rushed over the tangled roots in a constant current, the sound of it inspiring another verse of her song for Llyr. Between them, his erection throbbed in time with the pulse in her naked core and the beat of her composition clarified in her mind.

Even though she knew the arousal could be nurtured and

teased into something more pleasurable, she enjoyed the steady warmth that flickered between them. His aura was brighter now, his arousal a magnet for even more magic that as yet remained bound up in his restraint. Even though she couldn't easily see her own aura, she was certain if she looked there would be evidence of the same. Though she knew her task today relied on absorbing as much of that power as possible, she savored the slow burn that lingered between them and how it kept her musical muse primed.

He was her protector for today, but what about tomorrow? Perhaps after this task was completed and they were away from the overbearing scrutiny of her parents, she could convince him of the sincerity of her song. Yes, she still loved Ozzie, but she felt like she had barely scratched the surface of her capacity for love and wanted to explore every possibility there was. Besides, Ozzie wasn't here.

"It feels incredible," Llyr said, dipping his head to press a gentle kiss to her shoulder. "Are you ready for the next phase? They are waiting, and I believe you said you were only halfway to having enough power."

She sighed and reluctantly pulled away from his embrace. "I'm ready. Hold me like before," she said.

He nodded and splayed his fingers at her back, leaning forward as she arched until her torso slipped beneath the water again. This time he pushed his hips into hers and his cock pressed tighter to her core, the texture of the gauzy fabric between them a rough reminder of the promise he'd made her father. She inhaled sharply at the rush of sensation, but said nothing, only smiling up at him.

Llyr smiled back, though this time it seemed forced. His eyes swirled with both desire and the same uncertainty she felt tangled up inside her.

Deva sang again, but she kept the song light and unfocused. When she closed her eyes, however, she saw a pair of faces juxtaposed, and two songs merged. Ozzie's stormy gaze had haunted her dreams for the past year, reinforcing her certainty that they were bound together somehow. With her body lit up at Llyr's touch, a fresh, new desire took hold. The desire to have them both bound to her this way, both their hands and mouths on her, her body awakening under their ministrations. With the two of them, she could almost fool herself into believing that finding a soul mate was possible even if she didn't have a soul.

Aurum's skin tingled with the cool sprinkle of mist from the waterfall at the back of Calder's bungalow. She kept her face upturned, concentrating on the song that filtered through the air from the center of the Haven. The new version was different than Deva's first song. More restrained, less filled with joy and hope and love. The first song had been as lovely as the mating call her sister Belah had sung for her almost two years earlier, just before they'd embarked on the search for their mates. If Deva was finding love for the first time, she should embrace it. Sing louder, not hold back. Aurum would have to talk to her after the ritual was done and make sure she understood it was all right to seek what truly gave her joy.

A pair of warm bodies moved in on either side of her, every cell in her body shifting focus to the two men who gave *her* joy. Without opening her eyes, she could identify who was who. Calder's gentle touch at her back, his other hand threading his fingers through hers against the railing she leaned on. Nicholas's lips pressing against her bare shoulder, his dark hair falling in a silken cascade across her upper arm.

"It's time," Calder said. "Llyr says Deva is ready for more power."

"You are melded with Llyr, aren't you?" she asked, opening her eyes to look at her satyr mate. He stood in his full primal glory, horns glistening with the wetness of the mist, his features more angular and intense than his softer, human face. His cock was an immense, thick column jutting up between them that practically mocked her interest in anything but fucking.

Calder nodded. "The male Thiasoi are not blood melded, but yes, we are linked to facilitate swift communication."

"Does he know why Deva's song changed? She was singing of love before, but now the song is more reserved. I don't like what that might signify. Did you hear the same?"

Nicholas met her gaze then lifted an eyebrow as he and Calder shared a look. "Unrequited love, if I had to make a wild guess. I have been acquainted with that emotion."

With a worried frown, she looked at Calder. "Well? Does Llyr know anything about it?"

Calder inhaled slowly and closed his eyes. She observed him, avoiding using their meld to eavesdrop on his communication with his fellow Thiasoi satyr, though she got a sense of irritation that bled through despite not knowing what her mate heard.

A moment later he pursed his lips and opened his eyes. "My uncle's edict forbids Llyr from acting on any desire for carnal knowledge of Deva. He's in turmoil over it, but has camouflaged his deeper desire from her as well as he can for now. I can't believe my uncle did this. After hearing that song, Llyr is beside himself."

"He wants to make love to her?" Aurum asked.

A flash of pain crossed Calder's face. "He wants even more. I don't think Neph realizes how deep a connection all the Thiasoi satyrs have to Deva. I was only linked to her for a short time, but the other satyrs shared their blood with her for months. His bond to her is as deep as mine is to you. If I hadn't already had a stronger bond, I would be in the same state he is in. It's killing him not to follow through."

Aurum's heart swelled with empathy. She leaned back against Nicholas's solid frame when he slipped his arms around her.

"You're plotting something, aren't you?" he murmured into her ear.

"So what if I am?" she asked, tilting her head to look at him.

He gave her a devious smile. "Just wanted to say I'm one hundred percent on board."

"Do you mind sharing your link to Llyr for a moment? I'd like to speak to him."

Calder's eyes narrowed. "It is deeper than a simple mental link, so don't abuse it, all right?"

"How deep?" she asked.

"You'll see. Close your eyes."

She did as he asked, and a split-second later her mind was awash with the most intense emotional battle she'd witnessed in ages. The satyr Neph had chosen as Deva's bodyguard was holding on by a thread, his resistance crumbling with every second.

*"Help me restrain myself, please,"* he begged. *"You dragons have the power to strengthen someone's will, don't you?"*

*"Yes. I can remove your desire or enhance it, but I don't think that is the answer. Tell me the truth of how you feel first. Let me decide what must be done."*

*"Look at her . . . she is radiant. Until she sang that song, I*

*believed I could fulfill Neph's request. Guard her, keep her safe while she learned to embrace her own powers and sought out her place in the world. Now . . . simply being near her is not enough. Will never be enough. I must have her."*

Aurum's focus shifted and she looked through Llyr's eyes at the young woman whose naked breasts arched up above the surface of the water. The rest of Deva's torso floated just beneath, her arms moving in graceful arcs, up and down as though she swam in place. Through Llyr's other senses, Aurum was aware of Deva's legs wrapped around his hips and the uncomfortable intensity of his arousal.

Deva opened her eyes and smiled up at him, the variegated rainbow of her irises flickering with a golden light that flared to orange-red when her gaze met Llyr's. Joy, desire, and love were all reflected there, but so too was a shadow of uncertainty threatening to rise to the surface.

Aurum recognized Deva's dragon nature instantly in that look—her contentment to let the longing persist and linger, to intensify with each passing moment. There was satisfaction to be found in the low lick of those small flames, nurturing them without letting them consume you entirely. It was a uniquely draconic trait to bask in that simmering heat for as long as possible.

*"What do I do?"* Llyr pleaded.

*"Give her joy, but take your time about it. She is embracing her dragon nature right now, as she should. Encourage her by stoking her pleasure a little at a time. As her guardian, you are also tasked with teaching her, are you not? This will teach her more than you know."*

*"Neph insists that she's too young. I don't see an innocent when I look at her. I see a woman. My link to her tells me she is a woman. Yet my master's orders suggest I should not want her the way I do."*

*"Neph's an old fool who is too far removed from the complexi-*

*ties of youthful desire. Deva is more than ready both physically and emotionally, or else she would have never sang that song. Take your time, but don't hide your desire from her. Let her guide you."*

*"You're telling me to willfully disobey the Dionarch. Is Calder on board with this? You will back me up?"*

Calder's voice pushed forward, and Aurum receded into the shadows of her lover's mind as he answered. *"We will do whatever we can to make him see reason. Don't disappoint the girl. That song isn't one to be denied. No turul mating call is."*

*"Thank you,"* Llyr said, voice flooded with relief, and the joy returned with a vengeance. A moment later, the lovely song echoing through the Haven changed again, unfettered ecstasy rising over the crashing of the myriad waterfalls surrounding them.

Aurum relaxed and shook her head. "I hope we didn't lie to him."

"We'll do what we can," Calder said.

"I don't see why that wouldn't work. What are you two worried about?" Nicholas asked.

Aurum turned and cupped his cheek. "She has six other fathers we need to convince besides Neph. My brother will see reason if I lay it out for him. I think Iszak and Lukas will understand. Zorion and Zil desire nothing but her happiness. But Nikhil . . . He might be a bigger problem."

Nicholas grimaced. "He's going to be difficult to convince, but perhaps he's mellowed since Layla came along."

"Oh, good point," Aurum said, brightening. "We can divert his focus to our new niece and away from Deva. Perhaps that tactic will work on Neph too."

"My uncle is very protective of her," Calder said. "I think he fears the uncertainty surrounding her nature. Meri's intentions for Deva were never made completely clear in her grimoire. Neph would rather keep her close and sending her into the world with a guardian who is loyal to him first is a big compromise. Hopefully it won't be too difficult to convince him that Llyr's loyalty to Deva is just as crucial, but we won't know until we're faced with that task."

"She deserves her freedom, however we have to secure it," Nicholas said, a hard edge to his voice that made both Aurum and Calder regard him in silence for a moment. He shook his head at them. "She shouldn't have to live with not knowing any longer than necessary. Calder was there for me when I needed him. He didn't try to protect me from my own nature—he helped me embrace it. I'm glad Llyr is there for Deva. I think we should do whatever is necessary to help."

Aurum wrapped her arms around him and held him tight. Behind her, Calder rumbled, "Good, because the first thing we need to do is send her our magic."

Aurum's body heated with the deep vibration in his gruff tone, and a moment later, her conjured gown dissolved as Calder took advantage of his tie to her magic and dismissed it. Nicholas chuffed his approval as he slipped his hands down her naked back and pressed his lips to hers.

She sank against him, humming into his mouth as he reached between them to unfasten the tie to his trousers. He let them fall and stepped backward, pulling her farther beneath the spray of the nearby waterfall. The deck of Calder's bungalow possessed several low, cushioned chaises situated near the falls, the occupants of the Haven preferring the abundant moisture for relaxation over the blaze of pure sunlight a dragon typically enjoyed. But Aurum loved the way her body felt sandwiched between her two lovers with the water coating her skin a slick film.

Nicholas fell back against the cushions of one chaise, pulling Aurum down with him. She released a joyous laugh at his earnest, eager look that transformed into pure hunger when she straddled his hips and remained poised there, looking down at him through wet lashes.

"Sweet Mother, how I adore you," she said, raking her fingers through his black hair and gazing into his brilliant green eyes. She looked over her shoulder to meet the ravenous gaze of the horny satyr behind her. "Both of you."

Calder made a low, gruff noise that was the closest she would get to acknowledgment. He fisted his immense cock as he rested a knee on the chaise behind her and dropped his other hand to her ass.

Nicholas reached behind himself to unlatch the back of the chaise and let it fall in a wooden clatter. Then he reclined, pulling her with him. Cool droplets from the waterfall trickled down her ass and between her cleft, mixing with the heated wetness between her thighs. Calder slid probing fingers along the center of her ass and lower, taking his time to explore.

With an urgent grip, Nicholas pulled her face to his and captured her mouth in a ravenous kiss. He released her head and grazed his hands down her sides until he gripped her ass, spreading her wide.

The cushion behind Aurum shifted with Calder's weight as he cupped her ass, replacing Nicholas's grip. His breath gusted along the apex of her cleft before he darted out his tongue, trailing a long, slow lick from the top of her ass all the way to her aching channel. He buried his face between her thighs, pushing his tongue inside of her.

She let out an involuntary gasp into Nicholas's mouth when Calder swiped his tongue around her clit at the same time as he pushed one finger into her ass and twisted it.

Lifting up on both arms, she pushed back, chasing the pleasure of the penetration, aching for him to fill her more. Nicholas took the opportunity to cup her breasts and dip his head to suck her nipples one by one until Aurum found it impossible to make sense of up from down.

"Please, I need you both."

"How do you want us?" Nicholas asked.

"I don't care!"

She was only dimly aware of some wordless communication between her mates before Nicholas slid up the chaise and straddled it, leaning back on one arm while he cupped his cock and balls in one hand. He bent close once more and kissed her tenderly, pulling back just far enough to run his tongue along her lower lip like a promise or some silent signal. Then he leaned back again and tilted his hips up. It was all the signal Aurum needed. She grabbed his hips and bent down, kissed the dew-covered head of his cock, then swiped her tongue around the tip, tasting the combination of his salty flavor mixed with the crisp, clean water coating his skin.

With a stretch of her long tongue, she bent lower and took his entire length deep into her mouth, rejoicing at the guttural groan he emitted when she began to suck.

Calder's tongue slowed on her pussy and the finger in her ass disappeared. He shifted positions, the silken fur of his legs tickling the backs of her thighs.

Her core ached for him and she moaned around Nicholas's cock as Calder rubbed the entire length of his shaft up along the cleft of her ass, through the moisture and then down between her thighs, grazing along her spread folds and throbbing clit.

Then he proceeded to torture her by pressing his tip to her opening and moving it in tiny circles, just shy of breaching the barrier.

"Man, you've got to fuck her. She's driving me crazy here," Nicholas said, and she realized she'd gone still with her lips wrapped around the head of his cock, waiting for Calder to give her what she needed.

Calder let out a low chuckle and pressed his thumb against her puckered rear opening again. "You're desperate for this cock, aren't you? It's been a while since you've had me in my primal form. Are you sure you're ready?"

"Please," she moaned, pushing back into his touch and quivering as he pressed his thumb deep into her ass. "More, please!"

Again, his mirth rumbled through the air, a sure sign he intended to torture her. After the advice she'd given Llyr, she shouldn't have been surprised. Her lovers knew precisely how to appeal to her true nature, stoking her fire until she blazed hot enough to combust, but never quite letting the flames consume her. Not until they knew she was ready.

"Is this what you want?" Calder asked, prodding the huge, blunt head of his cock against her opening and pushing into her slick channel just enough to make her cry out.

"Sweet Mother, yes!" she yelled, rocking back, but finding Calder's grip too strong to fight. He held her hips immobilized while he shoved his immense cock into her inch by agonizing inch. Her mouth fell open with a gasp once he was fully seated, his balls a cool pressure against her swollen clit.

Nicholas squeezed the back of her neck with one hand, gently urging her to resume her attention on his cock. She gripped him tight and slipped her lips over his shaft once more, his energy adding a tangy sharpness to the sensation of his cock against her tongue as she began to suck.

She nearly lost her breath when Calder pulled out and slammed back in with a deep grunt. Her body tingled with the force of his thrust, her pleasure growing as he picked up his tempo and began fucking her with pounding force.

"Fuck!" Nicholas yelled when she twisted her tongue around his cock again, sucking him with abandon in the rhythm her beloved satyr set. Nicholas pushed his hips up to meet her swiftly bobbing head, his cock grazing the back of her throat with each thrust. She couldn't help but emit a desperate moan when Calder plunged his thumb back into her ass and fucked her with it in perfect synchronicity with hips slamming against her ass.

She adored his complete surrender to his primal nature. Calder was typically attentive to her every need, seeing to her pleasure before his own, but when he was in his satyr form, he took his pleasure as though starved for it, and Aurum happily gave. Each of his brutal thrusts into her aching depths drove her ecstasy higher, and when he bellowed as his seed shot into her, she knew this was only the beginning.

She tightened her muscles around his cock, milking him dry as his power flowed into her. Slipping her mouth off Nicholas's dick, she met his eager gaze.

"My turn," he growled. Aurum only had the briefest inkling of the mental communication that passed between her mates before Calder wrapped his arms around her middle and hauled her backwards. She let out a surprised breath when she found herself upright against his chest, pulled beneath the harder spray from the waterfall.

Nicholas climbed off the chaise and stalked toward her, the hunger in his gaze reminding her of the day they shared at the temple garden in India before they'd entered the Sanctuary. He'd insisted he was hers for so long before she finally understood the truth. And now she belonged to them both, body and soul.

Calder brushed his lips up the side of her neck and nibbled at her earlobe, his breathing quick and sweltering from his climax. His cock was a massive, hard presence at her lower back, still ready despite having just filled her with his essence.

Then Nicholas was on her, his wet body hot against hers, his hands bracketing her cheeks and his mouth hungrily devouring her lips, tongue plunging deep. He dropped his hands and grabbed her thighs, dipping to haul them up on either side of his hips.

His cock found her sodden core instantly and thrust deep, his fucking every bit the claim on her body that it had been that day more than a year ago. "You belong to me," it seemed to say, as if she needed a reminder.

"No, baby," Nicholas rumbled into her ear. "Today's not about what we are to each other, but what we can *make* with each other. Open your mind to us."

Her head fell back against Calder's shoulder and he slipped his hand up her chest to cup her chin. He guided her gaze so he could look down into her eyes. His irises swirled with power, pulling her in, and she went, surrendering to the rhythmic, driving pleasure of Nicholas's cock and the pull of Calder's soul calling to hers.

With a rush like that of a drift, she fell, hurtling toward the center of the secret, sacred place their souls shared. Pleasure and love surrounded her, washing over her like a never-ending orgasm. Then Calder spoke her name and Nicholas slipped out of her, leaving her empty, but when he returned, he was not alone. Her body opened for them both as they pushed into her flooded opening once more, together this time, their auras one powerful bubble around all three of them.

The claiming was complete, and with only a few more slow, heavy thrusts, they took her over the edge.

Within that sacred place, their souls merged, and that was when she felt it—the bright spark of creation that lit at the core of where they were joined. Their souls coming together had done the unimaginable and created a new soul from the power of their melding. Aurum cried out in rapture at the understanding of what this meant. This new creature that blazed between them soon took root within her, the perfect symbol of their love. The child of their three hearts.

At the same moment, Deva's song resumed, returning to its original joy-filled tone and rising up into the heavens.

*Good girl.*

ower surged into Deva like an immense wave crashing over her and she let out a cry, her eyes flying open.

Llyr stared down at her, his uncertainty replaced by a look uncannily similar to the look Ozzie had given her the last time she had seen him.

"I feels wonderful, doesn't it?" he asked. "The power they're sharing with us."

Deva nodded and closed her eyes again, relaxing against Llyr's strong, supportive hands.

For the first time that day, she honed her focus and really *felt* the magic flooding through her. Within all that power, she found the love that created it and the abundance of pleasure that gave it potency. Of all her parents and aunts and uncles—of all the nymphs and satyrs and dragons and ursa and turul who had come into the Haven to participate in the festivities—they all understood that they could love without limit and accepted that as inevitable. She had witnessed as much with her own eyes when seeing her mothers with her fathers, but for the first time, she felt how much power there was in the bonds they had created with their mates. Those bonds were the source of all that power, not just the Nirvana they produced when they joined together.

She could have the same. And when this was over, she would take Llyr with her to the human world and make it her mission to find a love like that for herself. Whether it was only with Ozzie and Llyr, she didn't know, but she would start with them.

Even though she was born without a soul, that didn't have to limit her. Perhaps all it meant was that she had no limits. Her possibilities were as endless as the threads she followed through the bloodline in her mind, and she intended to explore every single one.

Gradually the most recent surge of power subsided, leaving her with the steady flow of lower potency power that had increased to a steady current as the day wore on. She was glad for the slow build of it, at least. It had given her time to acclimate to the sensation of becoming a conduit for all that magic. Not to mention the experience of Llyr's enticing proximity.

She sat up again, taking a deep breath as her hips settled against his. "Is this all right?"

He slipped his hands down her wet back, the gentle glide sending a buzz of warmth between her thighs. The intensity in his gaze told her the intent of his touch was far from casual.

"More than all right," he said, dropping his gaze to her breasts, then down to where her legs were spread across his hips, her core tight against his fabric-covered erection.

Deva's pulse picked up at this change in his demeanor. It was as though some of the tight restraint she'd witnessed in him earlier had dissolved.

"I don't mean to distract you . . ." she said, her breathing too shallow for more conviction. She'd meant to make a joke, a tease reminiscent of his earlier comment about distracting her.

"My sole purpose today is to focus on you, Deva. Nothing you do could distract me from that . . . Quite the contrary." He rested his hands on her hips and gave the slightest squeeze and pull, forcing her tighter against his arousal.

Deva let out a soft gasp and pressed her hands to his chest. Her eyes widened at the blast of pleasure that tore through her despite the rough texture of his sarong.

Llyr groaned, his brows twitching with the return of that desperate conflict she'd witnessed before.

"What's wrong?" she asked.

His fevered gaze drifted over her once more. "You are beautiful. I'm glad you got rid of the dress."

"So am I. It's ridiculous to wear clothes in the water, anyway." She slid one hand up to rest on his shoulder and trailed the other down his stomach to the top of his sarong. "You should get rid of yours too."

"Are you sure it won't distract you?"

She bit her lip and smiled. "I think I like this kind of distraction. It makes sense. Is that strange?"

He took a deep breath and let it out slowly, his tension easing and a more genuine smile spreading across his face. "Not at all. Your dragon nature craves the contact. It's instinctual, I think, considering the circumstances. Why don't you lie back again and sing? We should have another surge of power soon."

"Sing . . . the song I sang for you before?" Her pulse raced with hopeful anticipation.

"Yes. Sing me that song again. Your turul nature is clearly the strongest. I'm wondering if we can take advantage of that strength to awaken your dragon power more. Consider this an exercise."

She lifted an eyebrow at his suggestive tone. "What exactly do you plan to do to awaken my dragon power?"

He grinned. "Lie back. You'll see."

Nearly breathless, she did as he asked. Llyr glided his hands up her back again and leaned over to support her as she let her torso sink beneath the surface once more. Once stable, she arched her back until her breasts emerged from the water. Llyr's breath gusted hot against her sternum, making her nipples ache for contact. They tightened to hard peaks when she glanced down to see his gaze fixed on both dark mounds.

Just as the newest surge of power flooded into her, Llyr dipped his head and captured one stiff bud in his mouth.

Deva let out a soft cry and pushed up into him, reflexively grasping at his head. After a few seconds of delicious torment, he released her breast and glanced at her with one brow raised. "Good?"

"Yes. So good."

"Sing for me again," he commanded, then lowered his mouth to her other breast and flicked his tongue across the pebbled peak.

Deva expelled a breath, then filled her lungs in an effort to focus. She began the song once more, softly at first, still a little hesitant after Llyr's earlier reaction, but his continued teasing of her breasts allowed her to forget everything but the desire, love, and happiness that the song represented.

The pleasure of his touch perfectly complemented the flood of power from the water, and when another surge arrived, she trailed off, her voice disappearing into the canopy above as she focused on the increasing number of threads visible in the bloodline with each fresh inundation of magic.

Once it subsided again, she remained relaxed in Llyr's

grip, enjoying the languid teasing of his tongue on her breasts too much to move.

He pulled back a moment later, and she sighed at the reprieve from constant attention and opened her eyes.

"How close?" he asked.

"Closer than before. We aren't there yet."

The blue whirlpools of his eyes flitted down her torso and back up. "And you . . . How do you feel? Did you enjoy feeding your dragon nature a bit?"

"Yes. Is . . . is that all it is?" she asked, hoping that he would tell her no. As much as she'd enjoyed everything he'd done, she knew there had to be more. Her body's awakening had begun the year before, but until today, she'd never known how good it could feel to surrender to someone else's attention. Someone who desired giving her pleasure as much as she craved receiving it.

She tightened her legs around his hips and her core spasmed at the tilt of his body.

"We've barely even begun. Do you see my aura? Has it changed at all since we got here?"

She blinked at him, surprised by his mention of his aura. "You know about that?"

Llyr chuckled. "Of course I do. I can't see auras, but my link to you is enough for me to be aware of your desires. I just wanted to make sure you're paying attention to mine. What do you see?"

His aura had gradually brightened with each surge of energy, but was far brighter since she'd discarded her clothing. Her song had also affected it, striking it through with electric flashes of power with each new verse. The emotions his aura displayed were only visible in her family members when they didn't think she was watching. She'd seen that combination of colors and brightness shared between Asha and Naaz on many occasions, and it always preceded them disappearing into their bedroom for several hours.

"You want to make love to me, don't you?" she asked.

He nodded. "Very much."

She sat up abruptly and hooked her hands behind his neck. "Really? Even though my father said it's forbidden?"

"I don't think he nor I knew what he was asking of me when he made that rule."

"Are you going to?"

"That depends entirely on you. I need you to know what it means if we do. Because of the promise I made to your father, I could get in trouble, but I want you too much to care what he does to me." The more he spoke, the tighter he held her, and the more his voice pitched low and intense.

"I want you too," she said.

"Good. But I want to make sure we don't waste this moment. Your power is the key to this ritual succeeding. We need to use that."

"I understand." She nodded, though she furrowed her brow at him, waiting for him to clarify.

Llyr laughed. "You don't really, but you will. It's the dragon magic that allows all of them to send the power through the Haven to us. Your dragon nature allows you to absorb it. But I think they forgot about how potent your own power could be if we add it to the mix."

"You're going to help me do that?" Deva asked, then bit her lip, not wanting to ask the next question and betray her inexperience. She had only ever dreamed of making love to a man, and while her dreams were vivid and left her achy and quivering with need, they were trapped inside her mind.

"Yes. But I'm going to take my time. Mainly because drawing out your pleasure will mean more power at the end, but also because . . ."

He chuckled and darted his gaze away from hers.

"Why?" she asked.

Llyr reached between them and tugged at the knot that held his sarong closed. It came free and he pulled at the end, lifting his hips up as he held her to yank the cloth wrap away. "Because," he said as he settled back and pulled her tight once more, pressing her directly against the base of his bare shaft. "Making you come would be the highlight of my entire life, and I intend to make it last."

# CHAPTER 16

Sweet strains of a song echoed through the dense foliage around the hot springs as Ked slipped into the water. Old memories emerged that he'd have rather kept buried, and they'd left him melancholy, an ache blooming in his chest over his past mistakes.

A pair of slender, feminine legs appeared on either side of him as Evie settled on the edge of the pool at his back, gently stroking his shoulders and digging into the muscles with her thumbs.

"Deva's come into her turul power very quickly. That's a powerful song she's singing," she said.

Marcus stepped into the pool opposite Ked, his green eyes regarding Ked curiously. "Why the broody look, man? We're on deck."

"It's the song," Evie answered. Her massaging lulled Ked, but he still had trouble relaxing. She slid the fingers of one hand up the back of his neck and combed through his hair. In a softer voice, she said, "It reminds you of when we met, doesn't it?"

Marcus frowned. "Jesus, you aren't thinking about that night, are you?"

"Can't help it," Ked said. "I hear Evie's song in my sleep. Deva's magic is every bit as strong. That poor fool she's singing to doesn't stand a chance."

"So, she's in love. Today's the day to follow through on those feelings, if there ever was a day," Marcus said.

"I agree," Ked said. "But Deva sang a different song yesterday. Do you remember the one she shared with Iszak and Lukas? Unfinished, but no less powerful." He tilted his head back on Evie's thigh and looked up at her, brows lifted. "You heard it, didn't you?"

Evie nodded, then took a breath. "I have heard the other half of it too, and so have both of you."

Ked frowned and looked at Marcus. After a second, Marcus's eyes widened and he shot a glance at Evie. "Ozzie's song? The new one he keeps messing around with whenever he thinks we aren't listening?" He smacked the surface of the water, kicking up a splash that splattered Ked's chest. "I *knew* I'd heard that thing before. I don't quite get why it's such a big deal, though. You guys look like the world's about to end."

"It's a mating song. For turul, when we find our One, the song is complete, but only when we meet that person. Ozzie's been playing half that song for ages. Only for the past year has he started playing the end. The fact that Deva knows the other half is more than enough of a sign."

"She's his One," Ked said.

Evie squeezed his shoulders and then swung her leg over his head. She slipped into the water and settled on his lap, smiling. "Yes, she is."

Marcus surged through the water, a harsh scowl on his face. "Then why the fuck is she singing to that satyr?"

"I don't know," Evie said. "But mating songs don't stop

working just because the target doesn't respond. They're like a contract, whether they're heard or not. And their power never dies."

"Perhaps it's because she isn't all turul," Ked said. "Her dragon instincts might compel her to search for multiple mates."

"I don't know," Evie said. "The reason turul are forced to wait . . . to live only knowing half a song . . . is because Fate determines our mates for us. Our *soul* mates." She pressed her hand to Ked's sternum, her eyes bright with love. "You are mine. And Marcus too, simply because he shares your blood and a bit of your soul from when you marked him."

Sighing, she looked between the two of them again. "But Deva doesn't have that . . . disadvantage? Luxury? She doesn't have a soul. So I don't really understand why Ozzie's so messed up over her, or why she'd even be singing a mating song to begin with. To anyone."

Marcus approached the two of them, hands trailing through the water and steam condensing on his skin. "Maybe it's the blood that matters most. Those satyrs were her source of life for months." His gaze rested on Ked and remained there as he came closer. "If she's still infused with his blood, perhaps it's no wonder she's singing for him."

"You no longer care how Ozzie feels?" Ked asked. Though he felt his own blood link to Marcus acutely, his body itching to have the other man within reach.

"Oh, I do. But I also know how much better things could be if he's willing to share. I think I'd just tell him to have an open mind." Marcus stopped in front of them, took a shaky breath, and reached out to cup both Ked's and Evie's cheeks. "I can't imagine life without the two of you. If she's capable of a love big enough for them both, I don't think Ozzie should ever let her go."

Evie's expression softened and she wrapped her fingers around his, then kissed his palm

Ked, however, completely lost interest in the goings on outside their little bubble. The bright violet halo around Marcus's aura betrayed the deep truth of the pure, unadulterated love that drove his words. He reached up with one hand and gripped the back of Marcus's neck, pulling him down until their mouths met.

Marcus moaned and kissed him back, clutching at his shoulder and settling onto the stone bench beside him. Ked's skin tingled with the sensation of his lover's aura flowing around them.

Marcus was right. Love that strong should be cherished, and he meant to cherish his right now.

The tenderness of their kiss shifted to passion, the quality of the magic surrounding them matching. When Marcus moaned again, it was less desperate, more demanding. They broke away just in time for Evie to lean in and take her fill of Marcus. Ked leaned back and watched while they kissed, his cock a stiff rod pressed against Evie's hip. The pair clung to each other, their auras red with desire.

He loved the way Evie's aura always swirled around her like a little cyclone, as though she had a perpetual source of wind clinging to her wherever she went. Now that cyclone grew to encompass him, its power flowing across his skin and ruffling his hair.

Ked could watch them for hours, reveling in the way they stoked each other's need, drawing more and more magic to them. Marcus leaned closer, gripping the back of Evie's head with one hand. Ked kept one arm stretched along the edge of the pool, but moved his other to support Evie as Marcus bent her backward. He released her mouth and dipped his head, capturing one of her stiff nipples. Her breasts were luscious round globes, bigger than usual, thanks to Sebestyan still breastfeeding. Impulsively, Ked leaned down and swirled his dragon tongue around her other nipple, enjoying the way Evie sang in bliss.

Marcus slipped his free hand between her legs and she let out a little gasp. She lifted the knee closest to Ked's hips and repositioned, her gray eyes a stormy swirl of need.

"Make her come," Ked rumbled.

"That's the plan," Marcus said, his fevered gaze fixed on Evie's face. He darted a look beneath the water and Ked followed his gaze. His cock throbbed hard as Marcus parted Evie's folds and stroked her swollen pink clit with his thumb, then pushed two fingers into her.

Evie sighed and arched her back, trusting the support Ked gave her with his arm. Her breasts beckoned and he obeyed the call, lowering his head again and sucking each hard tip in turn. She threaded her fingers through his hair, holding him down as he pleasured her.

Out of the corner of his eye, he watched Marcus continue to torment her, slowly swirling his thumb around her clit while he fucked into her with two fingers.

Evie spread her legs and pushed her hips into Marcus's hand, meeting his rhythmic thrusts with slow tilts of her hips. Each time she moved, her hip brushed along Ked's length, stoking his own fire to an epic blaze.

When she began to sing, the ancient language of her mating song sent an instant thrum down Ked's spine, making his cock ache. He growled, and at Marcus's rough chuckle lifted his head to meet his lover's gaze.

Marcus didn't say a word, but his look of longing made it clear that the song affected him just as strongly. He dipped his head once more to her breast and Ked joined him, driving her to her peak in tandem.

Ked dropped his hand and reached to cup Marcus by one firm ass cheek beneath the water. Marcus tilted his hips closer between Evie's thighs, but he held back, intent on the task he'd begun.

When Ked probed and teased at Marcus's tight opening, Marcus groaned against Evie's breast. He shifted positions, raising up and bracing one hand on Ked's shoulder as he leaned farther over. The shift gave Ked easier access, with Marcus's ass now out of the water.

Ked released Evie's breast and inserted his finger into his mouth, sucking it slowly as Marcus tilted his head to watch, his tongue and fingers still slowly working at Evie's core.

Evie's song continued, the pitch and tempo rising with Marcus more intent on her pleasure, as though he were trying to make her come before Ked returned his attention to his ass. But Ked had no intention of waiting. Not when Marcus had presented himself the way he had.

He dropped his saliva-slickened finger back between Marcus's cheeks and pushed inside his lover. Marcus groaned, filling Ked's cock with a fresh surge of blood.

Evie shivered against him, her aura flaring with the swell of magic that filled her, signaling her impending end. She threw her head back and thrust her hips into Marcus's hand, her song hitting the final note which she held in a long, clear cry to the heavens.

Evie's magic flooded into Ked, but he didn't take time to savor it. Their purpose here was to draw it out for the rest of the day. He needed to have a taste of both his lovers sooner rather than later. When Evie relaxed and Marcus's stroking ceased, Ked gently lifted her out of the water and set her on the edge again. She reached out and gave his head a lazy stroke.

"Your turn?" she asked.

"Marcus, and me . . ." Ked said, grinning.

"He smiles!" Evie said, laughing. "I love it when you smile."

"The two of you give me a reason to. I think I like having a new memory to associate with your song too."

Marcus stood beside him in the water. "I don't think I've ever heard her sing it quite like that. I like it too."

"I'll sing it again when you're inside me," Evie purred. She leaned back on her elbows and lifted her feet to the edge of the pool. Marcus licked his lips when she spread her thighs, baring her wet folds to them both again. He glanced at Ked, a question in his eyes.

Ked tilted his chin toward Evie and smiled. "She's all yours, but you know what the trade-off is."

Marcus chuckled. "As if I'd complain."

Ked admired Marcus's toned body and the way his immense dragon mark shimmered across his shoulders as he moved to kneel on the bench at the edge of the pool. He grabbed Evie behind the knees and tugged her close, then bent low, pressing his lips to her core and giving her a long, slow lick.

Evie's eyes fluttered half-closed and her mouth fell open in pleasure. She rested a hand atop Marcus's head, the gesture making him stop and look at her.

"I could spend all day just making you come," he said.

"I know, but it isn't just about me."

She darted a glance at Ked, who was more than happy to wait until the right moment. The longer they teased each other, the better the outcome when he got into the mix.

Marcus glanced over his shoulder and grinned. He surged up out of the water, stretching for the bottle of bath oil, which he tossed to Ked before settling back between Evie's legs and aligning his hips with hers.

The moment Marcus sank his cock into her, the brilliant purple of their auras merged. Despite knowing he was Evie's fated mate, Ked still envied the bond the pair of them had. They had loved each other long before they'd known of his existence, and in spite of the plan Fate had for Ked and his siblings.

Watching Marcus and Evie make love put the entire ordeal they'd endured the year before into perspective. What they shared was what the higher purpose had been all along. That love was the source of the greatest power Ked had known, and being included in a ritual to share it with a large swath of humanity meant more to him than he'd anticipated. It meant he was capable of sharing more than just darkness with the world. That he had light within him too.

What would Aurum think of him being so maudlin?

He chuckled and cocked his head, enjoying the view of Marcus's backside. His dragon mark blazed as he bent over Evie and thrust into her, pushing her legs up and lifting one knee onto the edge for better leverage. The shift in position gave Ked a lovely view of Marcus's ass, his cheeks slightly spread and his balls swinging as he plunged his cock into Evie's depths.

Ked pulled the cork out of the bottle in his hand and poured a measure into his palm. He stalked toward his lovers and drizzled more oil at the top of Marcus's cleft. Marcus clenched slightly, then relaxed. He slowed his thrusts into Evie and let out a low moan of pleasure when Ked bent to tease his tongue between his cheeks. At the same time, he grabbed his own cock and slicked the oil over his entire length, readying himself.

Marcus and Evie both stilled as he stepped up onto the small bench beneath the water, resting his foot beside Marcus's. His other foot went to the edge of the pool just outside Marcus's, their legs brushing together. He rubbed his oil-coated hands over Marcus's ass, squeezing and spreading, then teasing his thumbs around and around his opening.

Marcus let out a soft curse, but before he could complain,

Ked pressed his cock to Marcus's oiled opening and thrust deep without warning.

It was Evie who cried out then, the push of Ked's hips having slammed Marcus into her, but when Ked slipped back out again and glanced at their auras, all he saw was a mixture of raw need, pleasure, and love, which only grew as he settled into a steady rhythm with Marcus moving beneath him.

If there was no other sign of his mates' feelings, he still had Marcus's mark, which shimmered a brilliant ultraviolet beneath his skin, pulsing with each rough thrust of Ked's cock into his ass. Ked traced the coiled scrollwork up and down Marcus's spine and across his shoulders, marveling as he always did that this man was his—this human man who he adored, whose body he claimed, but whose mind had remained whole despite belonging to an immortal dragon.

Ked could finally enjoy what he had, now that their enemy was dead. He could finally take his pleasure with his lovers without feeling guilty for the part his kind had played in their near destruction. For the past year he'd been careful, first letting Evie dictate the attention she received in the bedroom while she grew bigger with the baby in her womb, then for months afterward while little Sebestyan took most of her attention away from Marcus and Ked. The baby's nature was still uncertain, having been conceived while Evie was a prisoner of the Ultiori, but so far he was merely a baby the three of them loved without limit. Today was the first day since that allowed Ked to finally focus on loving his mates without limit.

"I love you."

Ked blinked, sure he hadn't spoken the words, yet he'd definitely been thinking them. Then he realized it had come from Marcus, who was looking over his shoulder expectantly.

"Did you hear me?" Marcus said. "I said I love you."

Ked's heart lurched. Marcus had never said the words to him. Not directly, anyway, and he had never cared because Evie said them enough for them both. He felt his mates' love daily, but knew the deeper bond was the one Marcus and Evie shared, and didn't begrudge them what they had. But to hear it said aloud was unexpected, and a shiver of pleasure coursed through him that had nothing to do with the tightness of Marcus's ass.

He gripped Marcus's shoulder and bent low, slowing his strokes as he pressed his lips to his lover's neck and murmured into his ear. "I love you too."

With that small but powerful confession, his pleasure surged and he let out a cry, unable to hold back any longer. He shoved hard into Marcus, his cock erupting and his magic flooding forth at the same time.

Marcus and Evie both let out simultaneous yells of pleasure as their own peaks hit. Ked bent over them both, chest heaving as he sought out their hands and finally found them —Marcus's with his left and Evie's with his right. Together his mates brought his hands to their mouths and kissed them softly, a silent acknowledgment of their shared bond.

Not just two, but three, bonded equally in body and soul.

# CHAPTER 17

"There is no need to cry, Deva."

The hand stroking her breast in light, hypnotic circles disappeared and a finger grazed her cheek. Deva opened her eyes to see Llyr gazing down at her with concern.

"It's so beautiful. The magic that they shared just now. Why was theirs different?"

"Because of what they endured. Marcus and Evie nearly died in the Ultiori prison before your uncle rescued them. And now the Void has found light in his life."

The sadness in his eyes made Deva sit up. She gripped his face and looked deeper, past the swirling eddies of his power, and understood. "You endured so much for so long. I am sorry."

"If I could go back and change it now, I wouldn't," Llyr said. "What I endured brought you to me. I know Fate does not have a hold on you, but perhaps chance or chaos, or whatever power is involved in putting us together, has smiled on me instead."

She slipped her arms around his neck and held him close, her chest still a burning ember filled with the love that flooded into her with the newest surge of magic. Unable to contain herself, she let the tears come, cherishing the way Llyr embraced her. Gently, he gathered the wet tendrils of her long hair and draped them over her shoulder, then stroked her back while she cried.

The warmth of his strong body sank into her as he brushed his lips against her ear, whispering words of comfort. His attention calmed her, yet he kept up the contact and whispers, voice growing rough, his need a palpable undercurrent. The caress of his lips against the outside of her ear sent a rush of longing through Deva's body and she pushed her hips into his, even more aware than before of the heat that had grown between them.

"Deva," Llyr warned.

"I want to feel what they feel," she whispered. "You said you wanted to make me come."

"By the gods, yes. But once won't be enough. Have you ever had an orgasm before?"

Deva recalled all the private moments she'd experienced in the realm of the gods, left alone by the one person whose attention she craved most. After passing through those gates, her body had felt different, more alive and filled with an ache unlike anything she'd known. She had touched herself, thinking of Ozzie and wishing for his company. With her own hands, she'd chased that fleeting fantasy and found the briefest moments of rapture that were still a poor substitute for what she wished for most.

Ozzie had only visited her for short periods of time during their stay there, then left swiftly as though being near her was too much of a chore. She didn't understand his aversion to her, not after he'd been so caring and attentive during her first day of life, but it didn't change how strongly she longed for him even now.

Llyr was swiftly filling another emptiness in her. There

was no substitute for Ozzie, but with this man she could finally find that pleasure with a partner. One she intended to keep.

"Yes, but only when I was alone. It feels much sweeter when you give me pleasure."

Llyr smiled. "As it should." He slid his hands around from her back and drifted his thumbs over her nipples. The light teasing had her core throbbing hot once more, an even greater ache taking up residence. With his bare shaft against her, she knew precisely what she wanted.

She braced her hands on his shoulders and gripped his sides harder with her thighs, lifting herself up and enjoying the slick heat of his shaft as it grazed along her swollen center. Hyperfocused on every inch of flesh, she moved until the broad tip of his cock aligned with her opening.

Llyr's brows twitched in the briefest flash of concern through his open-mouthed hunger. "You don't have to . . ." he breathed, then threw his head back when she sank down, taking his entire length into her.

Deva's body flushed with intense heat, her muscles quivering around him as she stretched to accommodate his girth. For some reason, she thought she should have feared this moment, and yet she didn't. It made perfect sense for him to be buried inside her like this, and it made even more sense when she rose up again and began to rock against him.

Llyr's hands flew to her hips and he cursed loudly. "Gaia's tears, how does this not hurt you?"

"Why should it hurt? Does it hurt you?"

"Not one bit, but you . . . When did you make love to a man before, Deva?"

She was lost to the pleasure but the barest glimmer of her old fantasy flitted through her mind. The one that kept her company all those lonely nights in the realm of the gods. The one in which Ozzie made love to her. But she knew it wasn't real. She'd only made it up to fend off the loneliness.

"Never," she said, then kissed him.

Llyr sank into the kiss like he was starved, rising to his feet and bending over her, dipping her torso beneath the water once again. He kept his hips pumping into her with slow, delicious strokes, the pleasure every bit as beautiful as the magic she'd absorbed earlier.

After several glorious moments, he slowed and leaned back to gaze at her in adoration.

"Don't stop," she said. "Please."

"Don't worry, I will keep my promise, but this ritual depends on us keeping our heads too. It is almost time for the last phase. Your . . ." He paused and swallowed thickly, then pulled fully out of her. "Your father and his mates are ready to begin when you are."

"Are you frightened of him?" Deva asked. She tilted her head back and found a thick root stretching across the edge of the water behind her. Reaching up, she grabbed hold to help support herself. Llyr kept hold of her hips, leaving his erection resting along the inside of her thigh rather than where she wished he was—still inside her.

"He is partly the reason I'm one of the last of my kind. Of course he terrifies me."

Deva's body chilled slightly and she frowned. "He was not responsible. He *killed* Meri and helped free us from her."

"I know," Llyr sighed, shaking his head. "And he is my hero for that, but that doesn't change the fact that he is a brutal, skilled warlord, Deva. Any sane person would do anything in their power to stay on his good side. Neph is nothing compared to Nikhil."

She released the root and swept her arms through the water to help stay above the surface. Despite the clear worry in Llyr's eyes, he slipped his hands up her sides again.

"So we don't tell him. Or any of them. We're leaving the Haven after today, so we can go far away and they won't be the wiser. They don't need to know."

Llyr's shoulders gradually relaxed. "I hope it's as easy as that, but until we are finished here, we need to make sure we keep doing our part. Grab that root again." He tilted his chin behind her.

Deva reached back and held on, then shot him a questioning look. "Like that?"

Llyr dipped down in the water until his shoulders were submerged and only his head visible between her knees.

Deva laughed. "What are you doing?"

Llyr's eyes flashed and whirled as he licked his lips. "Continuing my quest to make you come." His hands appeared once more at her hips and he moved forward, holding onto her backside and lifting her up out of the water. Her knees came to rest on his shoulders as they emerged, and he pressed a kiss to her lower abdomen just beneath her navel.

Hooking one arm around her thigh and over her hip, he brushed his fingers over the glistening ebony curls that graced her mound. "Keeping to the ursa style?" he asked, lifting his eyes to hers while his fingers continued a light dance across her folds, as though petting her.

"Is that okay? I like how it looks against my skin. Do you want me more like a nymph?"

"You can style your yoni however you wish, but I would like to point out that you are part nymph. Perhaps experimentation is in order? The dragons are also mostly hairless. The turul and ursa like the wild look. Did Ozzie like you like this?"

Her body heated at the suggestion of Ozzie inspecting her nethers with such interest. "I didn't . . . We have never . . ." She trailed off, not sure how to answer, because she believed he *would* like her this way, though she had no idea how she knew. But Llyr was right; she should experiment to see what *she* liked.

She released her grip on the root above her and reached between her legs. Holding her hand over her mound, she closed her eyes and focused, using the nominal power she possessed to change the appearance of that small, delicate part of her. When she took her hand away, the coolness of the water lapped at her bare skin and she gasped at the sensual nature of the change. It was a stark contrast to the heat that bloomed in her core, which only grew when Llyr's gaze flicked down.

"Beautiful. Every inch of you is beautiful. May I taste you?" His eyes met hers once more and her core positively yearned for his mouth.

"Yes. Please," she breathed, grabbing hold of the root again and gripping it hard. He squeezed her hips and shifted his hands beneath her ass, lifting her up, then lowered his head and pressed his lips to the top of her cleft in a velvety, decadent kiss.

He remained like that for a second, his eyes closed. Then his eyelids lifted and a wicked gleam flashed as he met her transfixed gaze. He parted his lips and the hot, wet tip of his tongue snuck out, toying at the very top of her cleft, then slowly moving lower.

As Deva watched, he tilted his head, moving his luscious mouth over her now naked lower lips in a semblance of a kiss that was beautiful despite its lewdness. He darted his tongue between her folds in delicious little flicks, seeming to gauge her reaction each time he delved deeper until Deva lost herself and could no longer focus. When he wrapped his lips around her clit and sucked, she cried out, arching her back and bucking her hips up into him.

Llyr only chuckled and waited for her to recover before resuming. After a torturous interval, he hooked his arm around her hip and used two fingers to spread her open. This time he targeted her clit directly, swirling his tongue in tiny circles as he slipped his other hand between her legs beneath the water. He plunged a finger into her, fucking in and out while he drove her pleasure even higher with his tongue.

Just when she thought she'd break, he stopped and surged out of the water, looming over her.

"Why did you stop? I was so close."

"Because you were close," he said. "This is a marathon. We need to pace ourselves. I need to feel you again to keep up."

He pushed her thighs wide and slipped between them, his cockhead a more than welcome pressure between her thighs. He pushed into her, easing the longing he'd left her with. His cock was a comfortable, stretching presence, and she sighed as he reached down and lifted her close, holding her tight and kissing her deep as she sank farther down his length.

Deva opened her eyes to observe his expression and caught the pulsing glow of deep red and vibrant purple in his aura. Soon it rose to a brilliant, almost blinding radiance, and he abruptly pulled out of her, his chest heaving as he set her down in the water.

"Sweet fuck, I don't see how dragons do it," he muttered. "How do you feel?"

"Ready to explode," she said.

"Good. Hold onto that. Come back over here." He shifted backward to the ledge of roots he'd been resting on earlier and pulled her with him. She settled back on his lap like before, wanting him inside her but understanding that for them to contribute the most power possible to this ritual, they must torture themselves a little longer.

"Are they ready?" she asked. She was strangely grateful for the less carnal nature of their contact while she prepared to receive the magic from the next phase. She didn't think any of her parents could know what she and Llyr were doing, but it made it easier to focus if she didn't have to worry about what her father Nikhil might think.

Besides, she knew what *they* were all doing, and despite her age she was a grown woman with as much of a right to pleasure as all of them.

Llyr's gaze was fixed in the distance as she settled back on his lap. He seemed pensive, his lips tilted into a frown and his bearing stiff. Deva squeezed his shoulders, then slipped her hands to his cheeks and turned his head to meet his eyes.

"We can drift away as soon as it's done. You can send a message to Calder, and he can relay it to Neph. Explore the world with me, Llyr."

He forced a smile and nodded. "I would love that. We should find Ozzie first, though. I don't like the idea of keeping you from him if the two of you share a bond like we do. I can sense it . . . your longing for him."

Her heart jumped into her throat at the offer. Could Llyr talk sense into Ozzie? Make him understand how much he meant to her?

"I would like that." She would *love* that.

At his urging, she lay back and relaxed against his supporting hands. He didn't tease her this time, which made her aching all the harder to endure when the magic flooded into the pool once again, inundating her with pure, raw power like nothing she had felt before.

# CHAPTER 18

"Are you sure these will hold?" Iszak said, twisting a vine around his hand from the collection of loose green tendrils dangling from the lattice roof above them.

"They are Haven vines," Belah said. "Not even dragon fire can break them." She was giddy over the afternoon she and her mates had planned. For the first time in ages, they had the freedom to unleash their true desires. Lukas was busy lighting fragrant candles around the room, though "room" was a rather loose term for the cage they stood within.

Nikhil stared at their surroundings dubiously. "You say this was one of their prison cells? Fancy prison, if you ask me."

"They never really took literal prisoners," Belah said. "These cages are for . . . entertainment purposes."

"Nyx's episode notwithstanding," Lukas chuckled.

"And the vines . . ." Nikhil said, stepping up beside Iszak and tugging on one. "They are linked to the Source?"

"Every plant here is," Belah said. "Every ounce of magic we share will be sent to the center of the Haven."

She was careful not to remind Nikhil who it was going to.

There was no sense rubbing his nose in the fact that his daughter was at the very center of this ritual. He was grouchy enough after hearing her singing off and on for the past couple hours. Belah shared a look with Iszak and Lukas, who both lifted their brows helplessly.

"I'm not a fucking idiot," Nikhil grumbled. "And I can tell you three are keeping something from me. It's about Deva, isn't it?" He leveled an intense stare at each of them in turn. "Does it have something to do with that song she keeps singing?"

Iszak and Lukas looked at each other, and Belah sensed Nikhil's anger rising, his aura flashing with a fiery red that indicated rage rather than lust.

"Spill or nobody's getting tied up and whipped," he said, spearing Belah with a ferocious, yet subtly playful glare.

Belah hesitated, her brows drawing together as she tried to decide what to say. In one fluid movement, Nikhil stepped toward her, grabbed one of the lengths of vine, and wrapped it around her neck.

"You will obey me today, little beast," he commanded. His voice resonated with the promise of the pain she so loved. Both Iszak and Lukas tensed, their gazes fixed to her as she bowed her head. In her periphery, their auras flared. Nikhil's still burned with his demand, at the very precipice of rage that she knew could easily be diverted into passion he would take out on her body in the best possible way.

"Speak," he said, loosening the binding around her neck.

Belah blinked up at him and obeyed. "Deva is singing a mating song. That's all."

Nikhil shot a look between Iszak and Lukas. "Is this true? I hear her singing all the time and this song sounds no different. When did this start?"

"When she returned from the realm of the gods with Ozzie," Iszak said. "We believe she has fallen for him."

"Ozzie isn't in the Haven today," Nikhil said. "Yet she still sings?"

Lukas snorted. "Iszak and I sang our song for decades before Belah was even in the picture."

Belah stared up at her mate, hoping he would accept the excuses Iszak and Lukas made. She knew he could hear a lie if they told him one, and so did they. She was also sure they knew the song Deva now sang had nothing to do with Ozzie. But Nikhil lacked the turul talent for musical recognition. They'd tried to get him to sing with them or play instruments, but concluded that he was better at commanding an army and wielding a weapon than singing or playing guitar. So Nikhil and Ked both watched their shows from the crowd, with Marcus beside them urging the broody men to cheer the band once in a while.

Nikhil was far from cheering now, and Belah was certain that if he knew Deva sang for the satyr she was with, that poor satyr's remaining moments on Earth would be numbered in the single digits. Ozzie, on the other hand, was safely outside the Haven, and with any luck by the time they saw him again, she and her turul mates would have time to calm Nikhil down.

"We should not have let her remain with him for so long in the realm of the gods," he grunted. "I believed she was safer there while we sorted out the carnage after the war. Does he return her feelings?"

"She was safer, my love. Ozzie adores her whether or not he returns her feelings. He would never hurt her." Belah grasped his wrists and squeezed to emphasize her words. "He is also terrified of you. Please don't go after him when we leave here. It would serve no purpose but to make your daughter hate you."

Nikhil clenched his jaw, the vein in his temple throbbing. Gradually his aura calmed a tiny bit and he gave a quick jerk of his head. "Fine, but the bastard had better stay away from her or I'll give him a reason to be terrified of me."

"My guess is he stayed away today for that very reason," Lukas said.

The strains of music that filled the air faded, and with it the remaining tension in Nikhil's bearing. He tilted his head and smiled at Belah, a wicked glint in his eyes. "You are particularly obedient today, little beast. Does that mean you're ready to play?

He handed the end of the vine he held to Iszak and lifted a hand, tracing the upraised scars that graced her chest. His name, written in the curving, graceful script of his birthplace. The place where she had found him. Belah shivered under his touch, remembering the pleasure he'd given her a little over a year ago on the day he'd carved those characters into her skin.

"You remember, don't you?" he said in a low voice.

"Yes," she whispered.

"I have the blade. Our dagger."

Belah understood his suggestion but shook her head. Ever since their daughter Layla had come into the world, she'd gradually lost interest in many of the games they played. Even with the freedom of a new setting and knowing Layla was safe in the Sanctuary, she didn't crave the dangerous rush she got when he cut her. And though the sensation of hands or ropes around her throat heightened her desire to unbearable proportions, she no longer sought the oblivion she once had by having him choke her.

"No. I just need the three of you. That's all."

Beside her Iszak let out an audible breath and Nikhil closed his eyes, nodding. Despite their sadistic natures, neither of them enjoyed the idea of harming her to the point of death, even if they knew they could never actually kill her.

Yet they would have done anything to please her, and for that she loved them dearly.

Nikhil reached behind her and tested the vine that extended from her neck to the latticework of branches above them. The living tendril was securely connected and would not come free. He retrieved the end of it from Iszak and wrapped it once more around her neck, leaving the remaining length dangling down between her breasts against the vibrant blue silk of her gown.

Then he stepped back, lifted the hem of his t-shirt, and peeled it off over his head. His marks bloomed with power, the bands around his neck and wrists brightening with the desire Belah could easily sense through the link they shared as mates.

Lukas and Iszak followed his lead, each of them also stripping out of their shirts, their own matching marks on the sides of their necks flashing with brilliant blue magic.

"Tear off her clothes," Nikhil commanded, his gaze dark and utterly calm. He wasn't even aroused, though when Iszak and Lukas stepped closer, their desire was palpable as their auras merged with hers.

Lukas began to slip a strap off her shoulder when Nikhil made a tutting sound with his tongue. Both the turul stopped and looked at him.

"I said *tear off her clothes*. Don't be gentle about it. We won't be bleeding her today or taking her to the place she goes when I steal her breath completely. Those acts will remain in the past with the creature who made her hate me for so long. But we will not be gentle with her today." In a softer voice, he said, "And I don't think you want us to be gentle, do you, little beast?"

Belah's heartbeat echoed in her ears, mirrored in the steady throb between her thighs. "No," she rasped.

"Gotcha," Iszak said, and in unison he and Lukas twisted

their fists in the silk that covered her breasts and yanked hard. The wrenching of fabric jarred her body, jolting her backward a few inches, but the vine around her neck held her, constricting her just enough for her adrenaline to spike deliciously.

Her breasts sprang free as the fabric ripped down the center all the way to her navel. They switched to the back and again tore down the center until cool, damp air flowed across her ass. At Nikhil's command, they bent to finish the job, turning her gown into a pile of rags by the time they were done.

"Bind her wrists with the scraps," Nikhil said. He had barely moved, still watching her with detached interest, his attention as much on the pair of turul as on her.

Iszak and Lukas had adapted quickly to Nikhil's command, obeying him without question. Even during their private, intimate moments, they seemed to understand that seeking Nikhil's pleasure would by extension fulfill their own, and he never disappointed them. Even Iszak, who had bristled at the idea of being dominated by another male at first, had allowed Nikhil to direct him when Belah was at the center of the three men.

Now her beloved turul musician took the torn remnants of her dress and carefully wrapped her wrists in twisted knots she was sure were far more elaborate than they felt. She could have easily broken free—it was a conjured dress, after all, and she could dissolve the fabric with a thought if she chose—but where would the fun be in that?

"Are you ready for pain, *Tilahatan?*" Nikhil asked, lowering his voice as he took a step toward her and reached out, grazing his finger up the curve of her breast just beneath her nipple. He traced a nail in a small arc along the edge of her areola, just hard enough for her to feel. She let out a small moan, reminded of the pain of the dagger when it had sliced her for the first time on their wedding night and he had bent to suck at her nipple, lapping up the blood that spilled from the cut before it healed.

"We will find new ways to torment you, my love, I promise," he said, seeming to understand what she was thinking.

He flicked his eyes to the side and nodded almost imperceptibly. Iszak and Lukas returned to flank him. Both men sported immense bulges in their jeans and glints in their eyes. Her pulse raced in anticipation of whatever delicious torture the three of them had planned.

Nikhil himself still seemed unaroused, which bothered her. Had Deva's singing affected him that much?

He dropped his hands to her breasts, cupped them, and grazed his thumbs over her nipples in a distracted caress. Then his marks flashed, his aura flared, and he grabbed both her nipples between thumbs and forefingers and pinched hard.

She let out a surprised cry at the spike of pain. Her core instantly flashed with heat and renewed wetness. His groin swelled, stretching the front of his jeans to the limit of his zipper.

Releasing her, he barked, "Now!"

Both Iszak and Lukas stepped toward her, each one cupping a breast. They bent to tease her sore nipples with their tongues, tiny sparks of electricity arcing into her where they touched. She nearly missed the silver glint of the needles they each produced. All the air left her lungs and her entire body quaked with exquisite need that was soon met with the simultaneous spikes of pain through each nipple when they pierced her. She let her head drop back and moaned at the sensation of heavy adornments being inserted into the holes.

With another almost imperceptible nod from Nikhil, the

brothers fell to their knees. Oh, Sweet Mother, did they love her.

Lukas coaxed one leg up while Iszak supported with an arm around her waist. Then Nikhil gave her a lazy blink and a half-smile as he dropped to his own knees in front of her. Her skin erupted in goosebumps when his hot breath feathered across her wet core. With a gentle touch, he stroked her outer lips, back and forth with the back of his index finger, then inserted the finger into his mouth to taste her juices.

"Lukas, if you please," Nikhil said, tilting his head toward her pussy.

Lukas obeyed, parting her with his fingers. After glancing up and no doubt seeing her enraptured look of anticipation, he chuckled and kissed her thigh.

Nikhil was just as intent on pleasure as pain today. He dipped his head and darted his tongue out, hooking the tip beneath the hood of her clit and toying with the swollen, sensitive bud until she moaned an incoherent plea.

"I have missed giving you gifts like these, little beast," Nikhil said. "I think perhaps you've missed them too."

He took the proffered needle from Iszak, and with a deft press to the skin of her hood, he pierced her. She barely had time to enjoy the pain before it was gone and he'd inserted the golden hoop, a small, glimmering scarab dangling from it.

Lukas let go of her leg and she resumed standing on her own, driven to distraction by the new, yet delightfully familiar sensations the scarab jewelry gave her. Every breath made the ones at her nipples shift just enough for her to sense, and the throbbing pulse in her clit made the weight of that one acutely apparent. She could barely think straight when Lukas urged her down to her knees with a light press to her shoulders.

Iszak appeared from behind her again and she shook

herself back to full awareness of her surroundings. She didn't want to miss a second of what happened.

"You want to do the honors?" Iszak asked, holding up a handful of vines to Nikhil. "It's not exactly a turn-on for me to tie up my own brother, but watching you do it . . ."

Belah's eyes widened and Lukas grinned. "It looked like too much fun when he did it to you."

"He'll hurt you," Belah said.

Lukas shrugged. "If it's good enough for the goose . . ." He leaned down closer and in a lower voice said, "And between you and me, anything that gets a straight man to want to touch my dick is a bonus."

Nikhil chuckled and grabbed Lukas by the wrists, yanking his arms above his head. "I think what any of us are is about as far from *straight* as you can get." He leaned in and kissed Lukas savagely, eliciting a startled groan from the other man. When he pulled away, Lukas's lower lip was bloody and his eyes glazed.

While Nikhil bound the irreverent man, Iszak moved behind her, his mouth at her ear. "Not enough room here for a whip, so I thought we'd try something different."

Something cool, smooth, and flexible brushed along the top of her ass, then trailed between her cheeks. She tried to focus to figure out what it was, but couldn't. Then he leaned back and a sharp, stinging smack hit her ass just beneath the knuckles of her bound hands.

"Better than a whip, I would say," Iszak said, tapping it against her thigh before raising it up for her to see. He held a long, thin switch that had likely come from one of the Haven's trees.

"Let me see that," Nikhil said, tightening the last knot around Lukas's upraised wrists. He took the switch from Iszak, eyed it appreciatively, and without warning swiped it at Lukas's stomach. The turul flung his head back and cried out. The breeze curling through the place picked up. When he lowered his head, he was gritting his teeth and his eyes sparked with lightning.

"Still think you can take the pain, brother?" Iszak taunted. Another sharp sting hit Belah's ass from a second switch Iszak had apparently held onto, followed by a gentle stroke as he bent down and brushed his hand over her flesh. "Better to mix the pain with pleasure, isn't it?"

He dipped his fingers between her spread legs and pushed them into her. Belah moaned, her core clenching around his fingers.

"I agree," Nikhil said. He tucked the switch between his teeth and moved behind Lukas. Reaching around, he unfastened the turul's jeans and reached inside, pulling out his cock. The sight made Belah's mouth water and she eyed him hungrily, fascinated by the way Nikhil stroked him—hard, then gentle for several passes before stopping. Then with his hand at Lukas's neck, he pushed him forward.

Lukas stumbled forward a step until he was as close to Belah as he could go without falling over her. His cock hovered inches from her face, but she instinctively awaited her master's command before acting.

Nikhil moved to her side and threaded his fingers at her nape, tangling her hair around his fist and holding her head.

"Make him come, little beast. Don't remove your mouth from his cock until I command you to."

Holding her hair in one hand, he grabbed Lukas by the cock once more and aimed him at her mouth. Belah took a breath and descended on her lover, swallowing his shaft in one smooth motion. She reveled in the way his hips bucked into her and he let out a long, slow curse of pleasure.

Iszak toyed with her until she whimpered in protest. She didn't want to come, but neither did she want to hold off after being pushed to the edge, though she knew better than to hope for a slow burn from these men. She had trained them too well, and they were fully aware of what the ritual required. They would push her to a state of near-delirium before they let her climax, then repeat the process until they knew the ritual had been completed.

Another strike sounded and Lukas bucked into her mouth with a gasp, followed by a groan, his cock spasming against her tongue. She smiled inwardly. He was enjoying this too. She lifted her gaze, careful to keep up her tempo on his cock, as Nikhil's muscular arm swung down once more behind Lukas, and Lukas again jumped and groaned.

Behind her, Iszak alternated between short bursts of stinging strikes of the switch and tormenting her to the edge with his fingers before retreating again. After only a few more strokes from Nikhil, the whipping stopped and Nikhil moved closer. He dropped the switch and grabbed Lukas by the hair, pressing his mouth to Lukas's ear. "Time for something a little more intimate, I think."

Lukas's eyes widened, flashing partly with fear and partly with desire. Nikhil held him with an arm around his chest and Belah could make out the movements of his other arm unfastening his jeans behind Lukas's back. Nikhil only paused once to spit into his palm and drop his hand between them before plunging in with a hard thrust

"Oh, fuck!" Lukas bellowed, pushing hard against Belah's mouth. Her body thrummed with renewed need as Lukas's aura swelled to bursting from the fresh pleasure Nikhil inflicted on him, no doubt with plenty of pain in the mix with such little preparation. But it only took a handful of brutal thrusts before Lukas's entire body quaked and he groaned, the wind kicking up as his cock erupted and hot semen streamed down her throat.

She swallowed every salty-sweet drop, her body humming with the infusion of magic. Her turul lovers' orgasms always filled her with power that made her crave flight, owing to the essence of wind in their blood. Then a hand tightened in her hair and yanked her back. Her body torqued under the force, her aching breasts pushed out and her thighs aching from the stretch.

"Now my brother gets to watch and wait for his turn again," Iszak said. He held a lit candle over her breast and searing wax dripped over the golden ornament, heating it before trickling down onto her skin.

Nikhil had disappeared from sight. Soft splashes of water echoed through the space, and then her brutal warlord reappeared, glistening from a quick bath and scented of woody soap. His cock still stood immense and rock hard.

He strolled behind Lukas and gave him a swift, hard smack on the ass. Lukas smiled lazily. "That's what I like," Lukas said.

Iszak held her tight against him, the position forcing her thighs apart as he switched candles and dribbled more hot wax over her breasts and belly, and lower. He stopped just short of her mound and the throbbing ache of her clit, the heavy ornament pulling at the hood and grazing her sensitive nub with every quiver of pleasure.

Nikhil was taking his time digging through her old chest they'd carted in with them, thrilled to have an opportunity to use all the toys after letting them gather dust during her pregnancy, and then after Layla was born.

He returned with a familiar toy and her lower muscles spasmed, but he didn't come to her. In his other hand he held a glass bottle filled with her favorite oil, which he upended over the tip of the bulbous egg-shaped stone. The smooth, polished surface glimmered beneath the oil that coated it.

"That's not going where I think it is . . ." Lukas said, eyeing the anal plug with brows pulled together.

Nikhil chuckled. "I need to make sure you're well attended while Isaak and I take care of Belah."

Behind her, Isaak set the candle down and hooked his hands beneath her armpits, lifting her to a standing position again. He unwrapped the coiled vine, then proceeded to untie her hands and refasten them above her head. While he bound her wrists, Nikhil leaned over behind Lukas, grabbed him by the ass, and inserted the plug.

Lukas let out a guttural cry of protest, followed by a stream of foul curses. Nikhil just laughed and reached down, giving Lukas's fully hardened cock a little smack. "You love it."

"It's fucking torture, and you know it," Lukas retorted.

"What would be the point otherwise?" Nikhil grinned, then turned to focus on Belah.

His mirth dissolved into pure desire, his aura returning to a steady, red-gold glow. Isaak completed binding her wrists and she waited for more vines, but none came. Nikhil glanced behind her, his look carrying a silent command. The grating sound of a zipper hit her ears, and a moment later, Isaak's hot, hard body pressed against her back, his cock a rigid length along the crease of her ass.

"I have missed this so much," Isaak rumbled. He reached around and cupped one breast, wax cracking and falling away beneath his palm. He grazed his lips beneath her ear as he toyed with her breasts, tiny jolts of electricity sparking through the metal scarabs into her nipples, the perfect combination of pain and pleasure.

Nikhil fell to his knees before her, eyes filled with both worship and the promise of domination. He licked his lips and gave Iszak a small nod. Iszak dipped slightly, slid his palms down the backs of her thighs, and gripped her behind the knees. In one smooth motion he lifted her legs, keeping her upper body braced against his chest as he spread her open for Nikhil.

Belah's body ached for contact, yet Nikhil only rested there, gazing at her for several seconds, his hands mere inches from her core.

"Your body weeps for me, little beast," he finally said. "I think I enjoy making you wait, but tormenting you with my tongue will be even sweeter."

He bent his head and darted out his tongue, but only teased and flicked at the tiny scarab ornament he'd attached to her earlier. Nikhil proceeded to inflict sweet torture on her clit, never quite touching where she needed, but driving her desire even higher.

She let her head fall back and moaned, thighs flexing in Iszak's hands. Beneath lowered lashes she met Lukas's avid, hungry gaze. He licked his lips, but looked about as pained as she felt. Impulsively she exhaled a stream of blue smoke and directed it the few feet between them. Lukas inhaled deeply when her magic reached him and expelled his own deep breath in return. A moment later, she breathed in his magic and immediately felt the deeper link of their minds.

Within that connection, she understood how much Lukas loved everything about this moment: being forced to watch Nikhil and Iszak destroy her will with pleasure; not just enduring, but outright enjoying the pressure of the orb that filled his ass; loving every bit of attention Nikhil ever gave him, whether it resulted in agony or bliss.

Both turul men adored her ancient blessed mate. She hadn't realized to what degree until now. They hung on his every command, but not just because they feared him or even respected him. They truly, completely loved him now, as much as she ever had. It may have only begun as an extension of her . . . of the tie Nikhil had to her through the blood they shared, the part of her soul she'd given him. Their souls reacted to him as though he were their One as much as she.

But over the past year, she realized that love had grown and blossomed into something even greater, owing in no small part to how easily Nikhil had taken to their daughter. If there was nothing else she knew about her domineering mate, it was that he took his role as father seriously, and though Layla was biologically the product of Belah and the turul brothers, Nikhil considered her his.

"Do you want to give me another child?" she asked, her voice raspy with need. Nikhil paused and tightened his grip on her thighs.

He slowly lifted his gaze to hers, his brows creased and his eyes dark with lust. "Do you wish for another?"

She exhaled and thought for a second, sharing a look with Lukas as though testing his reaction. Within her mind, his magic only swirled with curiosity and absolute willingness to do whatever pleased her most. "I have no need, now that my family is all together. I have you—the three of you—and Meri is dead. I wish for nothing more. Except perhaps to come back here and do this again soon."

Nikhil's eyes brightened and he smiled. "Then I need nothing more, either. Except for this . . ." He leaned into her and pushed his tongue deep into her aching channel, teasing around her entrance in a languid circle that she watched enraptured and panting for breath. Her avid observation was broken when Iszak gripped her throat, holding her against him as his teeth grazed her neck.

Between them, he dropped his hand and grip his cock, rubbing the head back and forth between her parted cheeks, all the way from the bottom of her entrance back to spread her moisture farther around her rear opening. He only teased, but each stroke pushed her need ever higher.

Nikhil released one thigh and used the tiny scarab to pull

her hood back from her aching clit, then bent and stroked the exposed nub directly with the tip of his tongue. The acute contact was like open flame to dry tinder, and Belah cried out more loudly than if she'd been struck by the switch.

At the same time, Iszak pushed the head of his cock into her soaked core, the stretch creating a distracting contradiction in sensation. Nikhil's torturous licks made her body contract with pleasure while Iszak's slow, languid push stretched and filled her.

"Need to see you fuck her," Lukas growled.

She shot him a look. His entire body was taut with need, every muscle starkly defined and damp with either sweat or condensed moisture, she couldn't be sure. Nikhil chuckled against her core, but she sensed him shift, and a moment later her body rotated clockwise ninety degrees, with Iszak taking a step in the same direction. When they stopped, Nikhil lifted her leg a little higher, exposing her more to Lukas.

Iszak pumped into her with slow strokes. "Let's give him a show, baby," he said, returning his grip to her breasts and letting Nikhil take over holding her thighs while he fucked her. Nikhil wrapped his lips around her clit and sucked, drawing the bejeweled hood between his teeth and grazing the underside with his tongue, languidly toying with it until Belah was sure she'd lose her mind.

"Not yet, little beast," he said, releasing her and rising up, hooking both her legs around his hips. "Not until we're ready."

With a swift nod to Iszak, the delicious tight friction in her core disappeared, but she only had a split-second to miss it. Before she could blink, they both slammed into her together, Nikhil pushing his immense, curved cock into her slick pussy and Iszak shoving hard into her ass. It happened so fast she barely had time to prepare.

She cried out and Nikhil immediately began to fuck her hard, his gaze fixed on hers as he cupped her jaw. He held her head back so she was forced to look into his eyes. Tears streamed from her eyes but Iszak caught them with his tongue.

"Relax, baby, you're so damn tight and I don't want to hurt you more than necessary."

She had no breath to tell him it didn't hurt at all, but her body was too confused by the invasion to know up from down. It took Nikhil's command to jolt her into action. "Open up for us, *Tilahatan*."

She gave in, letting her body relax and trusting the pair of them and Iszak's clever knots to hold her up. Her head fell back against Iszak's shoulder as they fucked her, filling her body with pleasure from both sides and somehow understanding when to draw it out and when to push her higher.

Soon Iszak groaned. "I'm losing it. Fuck, you feel so goddamn good."

"Time to set her free," Nikhil said.

Across from her, Lukas rasped, "Fuck yes. Finally."

Gripping her thighs, Nikhil leaned back and picked up his tempo, fucking her with mad abandon. Her body jolted from the force of both cocks pounding into her, and a second later, Iszak roared and squeezed her breasts painfully as his cock erupted into her ass. His magic flooded into her with the force of a hurricane. He emitted a rough groan, but kept fucking, though he slowed and resumed his torment of her breasts.

"Come for us, Belah," he rumbled into her ear. Then he pinched her nipples, and at the same moment Nikhil reached between them and tweaked her clit, abrading it with his thumb beneath the heavy golden ring. She shut her eyes and bucked between them, overwhelmed by the surge of pleasure.

"That's it, little beast. Let go."

Her pleasure took flight with a sonorous cry, ecstasy flooding her at the same second Nikhil's hot seed filled her core.

They held her between them for several seconds, all three breathing heavily. Slowly Iszak extracted himself from her backside and stepped away to bathe as Nikhil had earlier.

Nikhil reached up and unfastened the vines that bound her wrists. He supported her as she dropped, easily lifting her in his arms and carrying her to the bed. He lay her down gently and kissed her, but there would apparently be no reprieve. Just as she started to get comfortable, fresh vines ensnared her wrists as the pair of them—Nikhil and a freshly bathed Iszak—bound her once more to the bed.

Belah watched, her body buzzing from the flood of power they'd given her, but too relaxed from the intense orgasm to react overtly when they released Lukas and he immediately stalked toward her.

"Fuck are you a beautiful sight," he said. His stride fell wide, reminding her of the object buried in his ass, yet he seemed not to care one bit, instead focusing intently on her.

He climbed onto the foot of the bed and paused to bury his face between her legs, lapping at her soaked pussy until he'd succeeded in pushing her desire halfway to another peak. But before he took her there, he paused and crawled higher, hovering over her with pure love and want in his gaze.

"The plug . . .?" she said with a lifted brow.

"Mmm, figure if I leave it he'll leave my ass alone long enough for me to enjoy you."

Lukas sank into her with a long, drawn-out moan of pleasure. Belah wrapped her legs around his waist and rose up to meet each of his languid thrusts. Despite being forced to watch and wait, he seemed in no hurry to finish, and when a whistle cut the air and he bucked from the force of a fresh strike to his back, all he did was grin and fuck her harder.

He came hard at the same time as Belah, but moved aside quickly. Iszak immediately took his place, dark eyes wild with fresh need.

He pushed her knees to her chest and hoisted her hips up, plunging into her at a new angle that drove her quickly to another peak with almost no effort. Beside her, Lukas lounged, He'd retrieved one of the many candles and almost lazily began to drizzle the hot wax over her nipples while his brother fucked her with abandon. She lost track of Nikhil, but it wasn't until the brothers had pushed her to several more orgasms that she reclaimed her faculties enough to look for him.

Nikhil was gone, and Deva was singing again.

"Untie me now!" she yelled. "Nikhil . . ."

The pair of them stiffened and looked around

"When the fuck did he even leave?" Lukas asked.

"And where the fuck would he have gone?" Iszak added, hurriedly loosening the vines around Belah's wrists.

"I know exactly where he is," Belah said. "You two go get the others. We need to get to Deva now!"

# CHAPTER 19

"I'm so close . . ." Deva struggled to maintain focus with the immense power flowing through her body. The bloodline fanned out inside her mind like a vast web of multicolored lights. Over the past several hours, it had evolved, first only with the dimmest silvery sparks, then growing in both intensity and variation until now she sensed the connections to several million souls, all of whom would receive her missive as soon as she had enough power to reach them.

But even with the most recent infusion, which Llyr had said would be the last full-powered surge of the day, she was still just shy of having enough. She tested the links, pushing what energy she had outward without releasing it, yet it still failed to reach the farthest souls from her.

Llyr held her tight, his arousal a potent, living thing causing his aura to hum almost audibly around them both. He had been completely still and silent for the last several minutes, simply supporting her body half-submerged, with his cheek resting between her breasts as though all he needed was to hear her heartbeat.

She combed her fingers through his wet hair and he roused. "What do you need?

"I need more power. Is there more coming?"

"All the strongest participants have given theirs already. It's up to the two of us now."

Her heart fluttered in her chest, silently rejoicing at his answer. "Then we need to finish it."

Llyr's chin rested on her sternum, his swirling irises flaring with power. "May I take you in my primal form? I can offer even more power that way."

Deva swallowed, remembering the glimpses she'd had of Neph and Calder on the rare occasions she'd caught them in their full shifts. It was rare and inadvertent; they seemed to reserve their primal natures for either battle or lovemaking.

As if reading her mind, Llyr shook his head slowly and said, "It won't be making love, Deva. Not when my primal nature takes over. Just remember that. I will make it up to you once I shift, if that is what you want from me. But for this, it will be a wild rut. You'll enjoy it, of that I have no doubt, but you may regret it. Satyrs are beasts at heart, after all."

"Am I not a beast at heart too? Four beasts, in fact, though I haven't yet learned how to unleash mine. Maybe your beast can speak to my beasts and help me figure that out." She tightened her legs around his waist, rubbing her sensitive core against his cock.

Llyr licked his lips and tilted his hips into hers. "Perhaps," he said, his voice taking on a richness that vibrated through the water and sank deep into her. He rose up slowly, pushing her along the surface until they reached a deeper section where it came nearly to his shoulders. "Hold that branch behind you."

When she had braced herself on a length of wet tree root,

he bent over her and latched onto her nipple, teasing and sucking until her core filled with fresh heat. Horns slowly emerged at his hairline in front of his temples and he grew in size. His hands at her back spanned wider, his torso pushing her legs farther apart, and within a few moments the water barely covered his hips as he towered over her, a hungry glint in his eyes.

Yet for all the change into his beast, she could still see Llyr. His face had grown more angular as though the skin was tighter across his bones, but his lips were just as full and his hair still the luxurious mop of curls cascading over his shoulders.

His cock had remained in perfect proportion to him and was now a frighteningly massive weight sliding along her inner thigh.

Llyr's lips curled into a wicked grin. "This is your last chance, Deva. Do you want me to fuck you?"

Her body was alive with wild energy, the urge to scramble out of his grasp and run almost irresistible. But at the same time, her core ached for the solid, thick mass of flesh to fill her up.

"Don't hurt me," she said, holding the root above her head until a knotty protrusion jabbed into her palm.

Llyr's gaze traveled down her torso as he slid his hands over her hips. They were wide enough for his thumbs to graze close to her core as he moved lower and inward, catching her lower lips with his thumbs. Deva gasped and bucked upward when he pressed one pad to her clit and rubbed, then pushed his other thumb inside of her.

"You have the sweetest, most accommodating cunt I've ever had the pleasure of fucking. I wish I'd been the first to test your limits, but there's no way you were a virgin. It will not hurt at all."

She shook her head, irritated by his repeated insistence that she'd made love to someone else. "I promise you're my first. Please, Llyr. I need you."

He pushed his thumb deeper and twisted it, rubbing the pad inside her against a spot that made her entire body flash hot with pure need. Tightening her hold on him, she dug her heels into his ass to draw him closer, but he was stronger and held back just far enough to continue tormenting her with his hands.

"I would give anything to understand what makes you tick. Why you make that claim when I know it's a lie. Do you genuinely believe it to be true? You can trust me, Deva. Your pleasure was awakened by another. I would bet my life on it. Just admit it."

Deva closed her eyes. She may have wished for one for the past year, but Ozzie had never come to her despite her unbearable desire to see him. She would have happily taken him to her bed, but that chance had never been given to her. Until today, the entire concept of making love was only a fantasy, despite how vividly her body seemed to feel every aspect when she brought those fantasies to mind.

"Just fuck me," she growled, at her very limit when he replaced his thumb with the tip of his thick cock and began to rub her clit in tiny circles with it.

Llyr chuckled and grabbed her behind both knees, holding her legs wide. "As you wish," he said, and slammed home.

It was all Deva could do to hang onto the root for dear life while he pounded into her. He was right, though. It *didn't* hurt. Not one bit. All it did was flood her with intense pleasure, and though she reveled in every stroke and jolt of excruciating ecstasy that flooded her, she missed the tenderness he'd shown her before. This wild, primal Llyr was dead set on one thing: fucking her to oblivion and finding his own pleasure in the process.

But it wasn't love that powered this spell, and she knew it. As much as she'd absorbed the intense emotions of today's ritual along with the magic from all the participants, she knew it was the magic, pure and simple, that she needed. The love that flowed with it was just a bonus.

She bit her lip around moans of pleasure, forcing herself to remain in control and fixated on the bloodline despite Llyr's steady thrusts, the teasing strokes of his thumb at her clit, and his fingertips grazing her nipples. She wanted to be ready to cast the spell to finish the ritual the very moment she had the power to do so.

Llyr's grunts grew ever louder, his cock a glorious pounding weight between her thighs, rubbing against every inch of sensitive flesh inside her. With half her focus, she kept track of his pleasure and her own, keeping the incantation on the tip of her tongue for the moment when she would need it.

The magic built with every rough plunge of his cock into her. Soon it was all she could do to withstand the pressure, unlike any she'd experienced when bringing herself to the edge and over.

As if by reflex, she opened her mouth and started singing. The song had no words, was only a melodic cry of pleasure to the heavens, released because she could no longer hold back. Llyr roared, his big hands tightening around her spread thighs, fingers dinging in hard enough to bruise. His crazed fucking and wild eyes awakened an understanding in her of what the difference was between what she imagined was possible with Ozzie and what a creature as wild and relentless as Llyr could give her, and she loved them both even more for that stark difference.

Rapture consumed her at that revelation, her cry rising in volume and pitch as their shared orgasms tore through her. The dam holding the tide of magic in check for the past few hours finally broke, all the power she'd absorbed so far paling in comparison to the infusion that came from Llyr's powerful climax, as well as her own.

The orgasms she had in her dreams were like this, and Sweet Mother, did she wish they all could be just as intoxicating. Her voice caught and hitched with the force of Llyr's final thrusts and she tightened her legs around him to prolong the pleasure. While the final spasms rippled through her body, she closed her eyes once again and refocused on the bloodline.

All the threads were there, even brighter than before, and she finally found the limit of their connections. Every last bright star of the constellations that made up Dion's bloodline was within her reach.

"I see them all now. I can reach them! Hold me, Llyr. Don't let me go until it's done."

She distractedly registered his immense arms wrapping around her and cradling her close to his body, his length still hard and pulsing inside her. Oddly the presence of his cock didn't distract her, despite how good he felt. The steady thrum of his pulse matched the pulsing glow of the bloodline and she realized as she studied it that it was because *he* was a part of it. She had known that, abstractly, but now it was clear. She could touch each and every mind including his with this power.

*"I feel you,"* she sent to him as a test.

*"I have always felt you, since the very moment Meri placed you in our care. You are so much more than you think, Deva."*

"I can feel them all," she said out loud, marveling at the way each glimmer responded when she reached out her power to it.

"It is time," Llyr urged.

Bracing herself, she gathered all the power she had absorbed. With the incantation in her mind, she pushed the magic forth, carrying the words she had spent the last day rehearsing.

*"We are the higher races, and we are not a lie or a hallucination. We are real. We are ursa, turul, dragon, and nymphaea. You are of our blood and under our protection. Our secret is now yours, and we must all protect the truth to keep our shared world safe."*

Along with the message, she delivered the spell itself—the one passed down through generations upon generations of dragons and used to secure unbreakable loyalty and secrecy from the humans who shared the bloodlines linked to them. They would be linked to her now, and to Dion, whose blood they all were touched by and whose powers would potentially manifest. Now these humans would know to keep their secrets close, but would also know they were not alone, that the higher races existed and were there to protect them all.

"You did it," Llyr rumbled, his big hand stroking up and down her back. Beneath her, his body gradually diminished as he returned to his human size, yet he felt no less present inside her, his rigid cock a tangible, pulsing weight that kept her core heated with need for him. It also strangely helped keep her focused on the bloodline, and she couldn't help but keep observing now that the message had been delivered to see if she could discern any type of reaction.

Llyr squeezed her shoulder. "We can stop, Deva. You succeeded."

"Not just yet. I want to see how they respond."

She was only half-aware of Llyr's tension, but with her eyes closed and her focus fixed on the network of souls connected to her, everything else was just background noise. It took several seconds before she saw the flickering glimmers she interpreted as the revelations hitting each of the tiny lights. They occurred in a beautiful, multicolored cascade from the point of origin—*her*—outward to the farthest edge of the bloodline she could reach.

"Oh!" She marveled at the beauty of the light show, her heart swelling with love for all those who were no doubt awakening to a changed world now that they'd been given the key to their respective truths. Even at the farthest edges, they shone even brighter now than they had a moment ago, and the feedback of awe and wonder warmed her down to the depths of her being. If she *had* a soul, it would be rejoicing now.

"Deva . . ." Llyr said, touching her face. "We need to move before they come."

"Just a second. It's so beautiful! Can't you see? All of them are so beautiful."

"Yes, and we can go meet each and every one if you want, but we *need to go*."

She sighed and nodded, but just needed one more survey of all the beauty she had been a part of creating.

But her wonderment was shattered by a bellowing roar. At the same instant, one of the lights went dark.

"Get your goddamned hands off her!" It was one of her fathers—Nikhil, judging from his choice of words. But his arrival worried her far less than what she'd just seen.

"Fuck. Deva, we're in deep shit."

Another light went out and Deva clung to him. "Something's wrong. Don't let me go!"

Two more lights blinked to darkness. Dozens of others flickered and dimmed.

Llyr grabbed her arms and lifted her away, pushing her back into the water with a splash. Her eyes flew open just in time to see him surge out of the water, thrown back by some invisible force. He hit the Silas tree with a heavy thud and grimaced.

"Daddy, don't! There's something wrong with the blood-line. I need Llyr to help me figure out what it is!"

Nikhil didn't even acknowledge her, instead pointing a finger at Llyr who struggled against an invisible force that held him to the tree. "You were sent to *guard* her, you son of a bitch! What gave you the right to fuck my daughter?"

"The ritual . . ." Llyr groaned. "Needed more power." Finally whatever force kept him upright disappeared and he slumped down and pressed the heel of his hand to his fore-head. "Fucking hell, that was unnecessary."

Deva swiftly exhaled a breath and covered her body with what she hoped were more opaque garments than she'd worn earlier. She clambered out of the pool and over the roots onto the patch of grassy earth beside Nikhil.

"Daddy, stop. I needed him. He isn't lying. I still need him. Will you listen to me? Something happened to them!"

"I don't give a fuck. He had no right to touch you!" He still didn't hear her. His eyes were filled with rage, his hands alight with brilliant red fire. He extended his fingers toward Llyr's head, flaming arcs dancing between them.

More figures came running up the path. Belah let out a cry of dismay, her other mates cursing as they reached them. Behind them were Neph and Aodh and Vrishti, followed closely by all the others.

"What the hell happened?" Neph yelled.

Llyr's brows contorted and he gave Deva an agonized look, then turned to Neph. "I am sorry. I failed you. I failed my duty, but if it gives me any reprieve, you must know that I love her. I would die for her, so if he wants to set me on fire, let him."

"Nikhil, stand down," Neph said, though his aura was no less filled with dissonant colors of anger and disappoint-ment. Deva ached with worry that any of that might be directed at her, but perhaps reason would return now that

Neph was here and she could explain to them what she saw once they settled down. "Llyr, explain to me why you blatantly disobeyed my order. You were to guard her, nothing more."

"And I did. I only did what was necessary to ensure the success of the ritual. That was my intention all along. But when she sang . . . Gaia and Dion forgive me, but when she sang, there was no going back. It would have happened one way or the other, but it *needed* to happen today for her to complete her task."

"Bullshit!" Neph yelled, his eyes swirling wildly with anger. Deva flinched and let out an involuntary gasp as his stature swelled into its true primal shape, every bit as glorious as Llyr's had been, but far more terrifying for the rage that bloomed in his eyes when he was full-size. "You were to tell us what was needed. We had reserves to tap into. Other participants. Zorion and his sister had yet to add their power. Dion could have given even more. What you were *not* to do was take it upon yourself to seduce my daughter."

"Didn't you hear him?" Deva jumped in, her body alive with anger at their repeated accusations. "It was my song! I sang him a mating song. It's my fault, not his!"

Neph snorted. "That song is a poor excuse. We all know your powers have yet to hold any potency. The only potential power you possessed was your virginity, which was clearly too strong a temptation for him. Did you enjoy the conquest, Llyr?"

Llyr pushed himself up to his feet, muttering under his breath. "She wasn't a virgin, so I gained no boon from being the first to make love to her."

Deva's skin grew cold, her chest tightening. How could he still say that? She hadn't lied to him.

"What did you say?" Neph and Nikhil both snapped.

Llyr lifted his head and speared both men with a whirling aqua gaze. "I said, she was *not* a virgin. She had no wellspring of power a virgin should possess when she first makes love. So either she was born without it, just as she was born without a soul, or someone got to her before I did. But I swear to you, I was not her first."

"Deva, is this true?" Nikhil said, confusion now a sparking addition to the crazed lights that flashed in his aura.

"No! I swear. Llyr was my first!" She turned to Llyr, tears springing to her eyes. "Why would you even say that? I have no reason to lie!"

"Don't you?" Llyr asked bitterly. "Would it be a lie to say you loved someone before me, that you sang a different mating song before the one you sang to me? Perhaps that one was answered too, and you are just ashamed that you were ultimately rejected."

"Deva," Nikhil said in a low voice. "Is what he says true? I will defend your honor at all costs."

"No!" she yelled, panicking at the accusations. "Ozzie didn't reject me. He just couldn't come . . ." Tears streamed down her face now and she hated herself for the display of weakness.

"Was Ozzie the one who did this?" Nikhil snapped. "I *will* destroy him."

"No, Daddy, Ozzie never touched me, I promise." She shook her head and clenched her eyes shut, her heart aching at how much she wished those dreams of hers were true. She wished even more that he were here, because at that moment, nothing but his music could have soothed her.

"Deva, that's a lie and you know it!" Llyr yelled.

With a flash of raw anger, she turned to him. "What the hell does it matter? All I know is that I can't trust you enough to protect me. Not when you won't even believe what I say. I had no reason to lie to you. But I have every reason now to never want to see you again!"

The Source beneath her feet flooded into her as though summoned, its power setting her veins on fire. A split-second later she let it pull her under, not even caring where the current took her.

$\mathcal{A}$gony tore through Llyr at Deva's abrupt departure when he realized his mistake. He had been too harsh, allowing his fear of Neph and his need to defend himself to cloud his judgment. It didn't matter one bit to him whether Deva had loved Ozzie first, or whether she still did. She had a heart big enough to love them both.

A heart that he had just succeeded in breaking.

"Where did she go?" Nikhil yelled, charging at him and slamming him back into the tree with a hand around his throat.

"I don't know! All I know is that she doesn't want me or any of us to go after her."

A worried Vrishti appeared at Nikhil's side. "We should let her have her space. All of you should be ashamed of yourselves for what just happened. She wants nothing more than to know who she is and where she fits into our world. This ritual was her chance to do that. I take it she succeeded?"

"Yes," Llyr said, his voice breaking over the lump in his throat. He longed to go after her and tell her he was sorry, tell her he didn't mean any of it, and ask her to sing for him again.

But he had been linked to her mind at the end, witnessed the web of lights which comprised the bloodline as Deva sent her power out to reach every last person and deliver the message. He smiled to himself, though he was near tears now. She had proved herself despite having no power of her own aside from what he could draw from her with his touch.

"You still must be punished," Neph said, moving to stand between Nikhil and Vrishti and crossing his arms.

Llyr nodded, ready to accept his fate.

"What?" Vrishti said. "Why? He really hasn't done a damn thing wrong."

"He disobeyed my order. It should not have mattered how she tempted him. He is a Thiasoi soldier, and he was given a task which included the command to keep his hands off our daughter. Failure was too big a risk to take."

The ursa shaman's teeth clenched and she jabbed a finger into the Dionarch's chest. "Don't you dare try to disguise the fact that you're punishing him for taking her virginity. That was *her* choice! And from the sound of things, one she was perfectly in command of making at the time! She did it to complete the ritual. Why, then, should we punish him for that?"

Neph's jaw clenched. Nikhil tightened his grip on Llyr's throat, glaring at him. "Because she is innocent. She may not know better, but *he* certainly does."

Llyr opened his mouth to object, but Nikhil squeezed and he couldn't take in any air, much less speak. He shut his eyes, hoping the other man would cool down. Likely nothing he could say would change his mind, anyway. Humans never did quite grasp the conventions of the higher races.

"That may be, but disobeying a Dionarch's order is still a grave offense. He must be punished."

Nyx pushed through the crowd that had gathered with Nereus close behind. She placed a hand on Vrishti's arm. "We will do no more than necessary. Trust me."

No more than necessary. If Llyr had any breath, he'd have snorted at that. He knew what his punishment entailed and didn't look forward to it.

A flare as bright as sunlight blasted his eyes and he clenched them shut with a wince. When he opened them, a beautiful woman stood before him, cloaked in fire and flanked by two men who could not have been more different had they tried—one a deep ebony with ultraviolet threads of fire beneath his skin, and the other bordering on transparent. He thought he recognized the woman, but it wasn't until her light faded that he knew her.

"Nikhil, let him go," Neela said, touching the angry man on the hand. A sizzling noise and the scent of burning flesh bombarded his senses. Nikhil cursed and abruptly released him.

"He needs to pay for what he's done, Neela. She's only a baby."

"She's a grown woman."

"She's a year old! And he should know better!"

Neela pressed her lips into a tight line and gave Llyr an apologetic look. He didn't quite understand why this woman . . . one of the three women Deva called her mother . . . should come to his defense, but he was grateful nonetheless.

"That may be true, but she is not a normal creature. You and I both know what Meri's experiments can do to someone. Just because she is dead now doesn't mean we have escaped all the repercussions of her acts. This very ritual was evidence of that, as is Deva.

"The second Deva was taken from my womb, we lost the chance to control her fate. Last year we learned that she may not even have a fate, due to her origins. Yet I have seen her desire grow to find a place for herself. She is older in spirit than her true age suggests. If you spent more time with her, you would see that.

"Next time you see her, just look into her eyes. She is a creature made of all our souls even if she lacks her own, and somehow her creation gave her wisdom far beyond any a woman as new to the world as she is has a right to. Yet she has it. She made this decision. Don't blame her for it, or anyone else for loving the amazing woman she has become. And be grateful that she was allowed to make the choice herself."

Llyr decided he probably loved this woman almost as much as he loved her daughter. When Nikhil finally did step back, he wrapped his arms around her.

"Thank you," Llyr said gruffly, barely conscious of the steam spilling off him into the air.

Neela laughed and pushed away. "I'm hurting you . . ."

"Nah, it's just steam. I'll survive. I would rather hug you than what I've got to do now, any day." Taking a deep breath, he turned to Neph. "Let's get this over with."

He stepped onto the path, resolute, then stopped and turned. Neph was speaking softly to Vrishti, who had Belah and Neela at her side.

"Is everything all right?" he asked.

With a solemn look, Neph nodded and the three women turned to go. "They are going back to the palace to wait for Deva. Perhaps she will return for them. It seems all the men in my daughter's life have failed her today."

LLYR'S FEET felt heavier with each step into the damp, dark cavern. It might have been an effect of the magic protecting the Diviner's lair from intruders, but he knew better. Punishment for his kind meant a bodily sacrifice to the creature who lived in this dark, secluded grotto cut into the stone of the Haven itself.

He would survive, but not without cost.

A moment before passing through the final barrier into the Diviner's cave, he let his primal shape take over. He would obey every rule given to him from here on out, even if it killed him, and that included arriving in his true form to accept his punishment.

The incline leveled off as the passage opened up, and Llyr was nearly blinded by the sparkling of brilliant gemstones that covered all the walls. The cavern itself was half again bigger than he remembered, and he couldn't help but stand and gawk at the beauty.

The others entered behind him in their various shapes until the massive room was filled with dragons, bears, nymphs, and satyrs, and a handful of falcons hovering in the air or perched on the nearest set of horns of their companions.

"What the hell happened to this place?" he asked. The only thing that looked the same was the shadowy mist at the far end of what was now an even bigger pool. Slithering noises filled the room along with the sounds of small waves lapping at the smooth stone edge of the pool.

"We helped the Diviner renovate a bit after Meri collapsed the tunnel last year," Calder said. "Which means she's been in a good mood all year, so that could either be wonderful or terrible news for you."

The slithering grew louder and Llyr took a deep breath, forcing himself to step closer to the edge.

A resonant voice reverberated through the big chamber, sounding as though it came from all sides. "To what do I owe thisss pleasssure today? Are you all ssharing your Equinox ssselebration with me for once? Ssshall we have an orgy here?"

Calder shivered beside Llyr, despite the thick fur that covered his legs, and Llyr's skin pricked into goosebumps. Neph stepped forward to greet the Diviner, his hooved feet echoing on the wet stone.

"The Thiasoi named Llyr has disobeyed my order today and requires discipline. Once that is complete, if it is your wish for any of us to remain and celebrate, we will happily do so."

The water's surface rippled and several thick tails appeared, their tips slipping past the lip of the pool and curling back and forth as though seeking something. Llyr swallowed thickly, remembering his initiation as a Thiasoi and what those tendrils did to him then.

"Only a year returned and a satyr has disobeyed his massster? How unfortunate." One of the tendrils found its way to Llyr's feet and tickled a slow path up and around his ankle. "What do you have to say for yourssself, Llyr Xanthosss? Wasss she worth it?"

Llyr took a deep breath and stepped into the pool. "Every second with her was worth the punishment ten times over."

"Then thisss shall be easy for both of usss. Come to me, child."

He dove in and was immediately surrounded by dozens of slippery tails. They twined round his arms and legs, carrying him across the water's surface, teasing and exploring his entire body along the way. Then they stopped and he found himself lifted up until a pair of huge, feminine arms held him against soft breasts. He gazed up into eyes so brilliant blue, he wondered if she had a piece of sky in her soul. The lovely face that looked down at him smiled, displaying razor-sharp teeth.

"I am one-third dragon, after all," the Diviner said, then

laughed, and the tiny silvery snakes that coiled and writhed around her head seemed to quake with their own mirth.

As if to demonstrate that part of her, she pursed her lips into an O and blew out a breath. Dense, white mist coalesced around them both. At his look of confusion, she whispered, "Thisss is between the two of usss, I think. Calder was right, I'm in a good mood. Neph doesn't need to know what I'm about. Besidesss, he did just offer me an orgy, ssso I may take him up on that."

"What are you going to do with me?" Llyr asked with gruff uncertainty. It felt odd to be held the way he was, cradled like a babe in her arms, but to a creature as immense as she, he was no bigger than one.

"Sssimply help you sssee . . ." With that, the tendrils reappeared, wrapped around him and pulled him abruptly beneath the water. He barely had time to catch his breath before he was submerged, but that wasn't the end.

Her tails caressed him with the gentle touch of a hundred lovers, driving his desire to a swift peak, then slowing. They tickled and teased around his cock, keeping it hard and aching painfully for a release despite the drawn out and very satisfying conclusion he'd had after making love to Deva. Then he remembered he had not made love to her and cursed himself.

*"You could have had a deeper meld with her, had you taken your time,"* the Diviner said, her voice as potent a caress inside his mind as her tendrils were all over his body. *"You could have given her a piece of your sssoul—something she craves more than anything else."*

"There is a way to give her a soul?" Llyr asked, latching onto her words despite the unbearable pleasure she inflicted on him once more.

*"Fate's hounds are blind to her and cannot hunt her a sssoul mate. But there are some that may still see her without Fate's influ-*

*ence. Without the hounds, the mate mussst come first, for a sssoul can only be shared through a melding of true love. Had you made love to her at the end, you could have granted her a piece of your sssoul."*

"I cannot be her soul mate unless she has that, can I? And there is no chance of Fate putting her in my path again if his hounds can't see her."

*"You must work for her love, Llyr Xanthosss, as must all who wish to share in the Chimera's power when she awakensss fully. And ssso you must work to find her if you wish to make amendsss. But you have an advantage there, don't you?"*

With that, her torment grew so acute he lost his hold on sanity for several moments, his body torqueing in the grip of all her tails. The tip of one was coiled around his cock, stroking him, another around his balls, tugging and teasing, and a third was buried in his ass, thrusting. She stopped right when he was poised at the edge of release, and he let out a vile curse.

The Diviner laughed and resumed her torture along with the mental lecture. *"I am part dragon, and you did come here for punishment. There is just one more thing you must know . . ."*

Llyr twisted in her grip, chasing more direct contact and wishing he hadn't said the things he had to Deva to make her cry. "What is it?" he growled.

She didn't the answer at first, but her torment increased. Her grip on his cock tightened and she pushed deeper into his ass. He climaxed with a roar, his head flying back, horns hitting writhing coils of flesh. Somehow she succeeded in pushing his orgasm to its very limit, semen erupting from his cock in violent spurts until his balls ached. His cock still spasmed for several more seconds after he was entirely spent and almost to the point of begging for mercy.

Nearly delirious from the torture, he soon found himself cradled again in her arms, oddly content within her soft embrace. Her breasts were a cushion beneath his cheek and he sighed, but tensed when she spoke again, this time her voice completely clear as it echoed through the big cavern.

"Fate's hounds are on the hunt, drawn to the scent of the magic of the bloodline. The god's blood makes the bloodline easy to track, and the hounds will hunt down every creature linked to it unless they are stopped."

Llyr's blood went cold as her tails drew him away from her, leaving him standing chest-deep in the water staring up at her. "Then we must go protect them all like we promised. How do we control the hounds?"

"You don't. Deva is the flame. It is her magic that draws the beasts which only she can see. But they are wild, broken free from their master's leash. They will wreak havoc if they are not tamed. They don't know the damage they cause . . . the deaths of the bloodline that are inevitable."

Llyr's mind spun, his adrenaline spiking with the need to carry out Neph's original missive: To protect Deva at all costs.

"I don't care about them! That whole fucking bloodline can die. We'll keep her here in the Haven, safe. The beasts will never find her."

"Oh, will you?" the Diviner said, bending down and staring him in the eyes until he felt dizzy and seasick. "And where do you suppose she is now?"

For the first time since she'd drifted away, Llyr tested their link, seeking her out. But it was stretched thin and faint, as though several magical barriers stood between them. He had no sense of her location or her state of mind. All he knew was that she was not in the Haven, nor in any of the higher realms.

Then he remembered her alarm just before Nikhil had arrived. Her insistence that something was wrong with the bloodline already.

"Oh, Gaia. No. Please tell me she didn't go out there alone!"

"The flame and the beasts will find each other, Llyr Xanthos. Unless you find them first."

~

Thank you for reading "Dragon Avenged"! If you loved it, please visit the retailer and leave a review!

**Ready for another epic story?**
Deva Rainsong's adventure is only beginning. Pick up "Fate's Fools" today, or keep reading for a preview.

And don't forget, subscribing to the Dragon Beasties mailing list gets you **two free sexy dragon shifter stories** not available for sale anywhere.

**FATE'S FOOLS**
**(A Reverse Harem Romance)**

**HOW DO you find your soul mate if you're born without a soul?**

Deva Rainsong is a chimera, a mixed breed of all four higher races, bred in a lab by the dragons' mortal enemy. She was meant to be a vessel to house the enemy's soul, but with the enemy dead in a recent war, Deva is left unclaimed—without a soul of her own and with a deep, cold longing for a love she doesn't think Fate will ever offer.

Five men have captured Deva's heart, yet she refuses to entertain the thought of binding them to her. Even if she could unlock her ability to mark mates of her own, she has no soul to offer a potential soul mate.

Love without a true soul mate can only be an empty affair, and surely Fate has other plans for all of them besides a soulless girl like her. But when the six of them embark on a mission to uncover the secrets of a pack of rogue Fate hounds, they learn that Fate's reach is not boundless, and that they have more control over their destinies than they believed.

*Read on for an excerpt, or* buy now.

~

## Chapter One

The ursa claimed that when they went on their pilgrimage as young adults, they did this thing they called "soul searching." I'd always wondered what this meant. Were their souls vessels that needed to be emptied like old luggage and rifled through to find clues to their true paths? Or were they missing their souls and the pilgrimage was how they found them?

I'd never asked anyone else this question because I kind of already knew the answer—their soul searching was a journey to understand the souls they already possessed. I liked to think my own pilgrimage was the same thing, except I was probably fooling myself.

First of all, I wasn't really on a pilgrimage. I ran away from home, and my family was probably looking for me.

Secondly, I didn't have a soul, which was a double-edged sword. It meant I was nearly impossible for my family to find, but it also meant I was missing the one thing that could probably have told me where I belonged in the world, and was fairly certain my quest wasn't going to lead me to it.

Ever since I left, I'd been going through the motions of this so-called "soul search," but I hadn't really learned a whole lot about myself that I didn't already know. I was an infinitely adaptable creature and a quick study, yet the powers I was born with were still wimpy as fuck. Three weeks into a self-imposed exile from the life I'd known, all I'd really learned were things related to the human world to which I'd fled.

Humanity was both amazingly resilient and heartbreakingly fragile at the same time. I finally understood why the higher races were so drawn to them. Why the dragons used to collect human mates and hoard them like treasure.

That particular instinct wasn't exactly dormant in me. Thanks to my somewhat unorthodox origins, I was magically linked to a special segment of humanity infused with divine blood. And thanks to that blood, there was something distinctly magical hurting some of the humans of the bloodline.

My deepest instincts urged me to protect them. Whether it was my dragon nature at work, or a trait of one of the other four races in my blood, I kind of wanted to take half the bloodline home with me just to keep them safe. That would have solved a lot of issues, but it wasn't exactly feasible to show up in the Dragon Glade or one of the other sacred homes of the higher races with a whole pile of humans in tow.

Even if I *could* go home. One of the few things I'd learned about myself was that I was stubborn as hell. I was part human, so that resilience and tenacity was there, but I was also immortal, and therefore not so fragile, at least not on the outside. I couldn't leave the human world until I'd figured out what was hurting the people I was linked to and why, even if it meant keeping watch over the one thing they possessed that I didn't: their souls.

The irony was *not* lost on me.

I'd spent the bulk of my introduction to the human world within the sterile hallways of hospitals, achingly aware of the suffering of every soul. But that was where the victims of these magical creatures had wound up, each one falling into mysterious comas for days on end. So far I'd only been able to observe events, powerless to do anything but hang around and wait for something to happen. Without a clue as to the reason for the attacks or what these creatures were, I had no way to stop them, so it was a waiting game.

Another thing I'd learned in those three interminable weeks was that human food was disgusting. I peeled the piece of bread back from the sandwich I was about to eat and narrowed my eyes at the blob of . . . something . . . beneath.

"What is this?" I poked at the brownish substance and scrunched my nose. A low chuckle carried from the next table in the hospital's desolate cafeteria.

"Catch of the night," my dining companion said. "Canned tuna salad is my guess."

I darted a glance at the man, heat rising in my cheeks at the realization that I'd spoken out loud. My heart skittered at his striking gray-green eyes, a contrast to the warm brown of his skin, which was no less vibrant for the weariness in his bearing, his unkempt hair, and his scruffy chin. He lifted his own sandwich in a little salute and took a bite, eyes twinkling.

"See? Edible." He took a second bite, and then his eyes bugged out and with an exaggerated spasm he slumped down with his face on the tray. His muscular forearms bracketed his head, both covered in mesmerizing, colorful designs that stretched from wrists all the way up past the sleeves of his plain threadbare t-shirt.

I lifted my eyebrows. He opened one eye, narrowed it at me, then sat up and finished chewing.

"No reaction, huh? Tough crowd."

"You were faking, but nice try?" It was tough to be surprised when his intentions blazed in his aura clear as day —just as clear as the telltale orb of light inside his chest. His soul possessed a particular quality that gave him away as a member of the bloodline I'd taken it upon myself to watch over.

Still, I probably should have laughed. He'd just surprised

me, and my interpersonal skills were still . . . well, *rough* would be an understatement. I knew how to act around family, but my family wasn't exactly human. This cute, tattooed guy's humor was new to me.

"I've seen you around the last two weeks. Are you a doctor?" he asked, apparently giving up on attempting to make me laugh. I kind of wished he'd try again so I could do it right the second time.

"No," I said. "I think they eat in a separate cafeteria, anyway." I waited and hoped he'd follow through on the recognition that always came when a new member of the bloodline finally registered what I was.

This particular man was someone I'd watched for the past two weeks, ever since his arrival with a sick elderly woman. Humans were fragile creatures, but her fragility had very little to do with her humanity or age and everything to do with why I couldn't go home yet, even if I'd wanted to.

But so far I'd only watched him from a safe distance, protected by the bounds of human social customs—and the hospital's visitation policies. Now that he was talking to me, I was painfully aware of his attention. Until now I hadn't realized how much I'd *missed* simple conversation, but more than that, I missed *contact* so much I ached for it.

He'd stopped eating and was now just staring at me. I took a bite of my sandwich and pretended not to notice. I knew better than to push, despite how giddy the sound of his voice made me. It would be easier if I let him start the conversation.

The bloodline were the only members of humanity who knew about my kind, and they'd only just discovered our existence. Despite the efforts the higher races had taken to clue them in, most of them still seemed pretty damn oblivious, or at least selectively blind. Another thing I'd learned about humanity was that they were incredibly adept at denial, even when they had more than enough evidence of the truth.

"Discovered" was probably a strong word, though; the bloodline had already been on the verge of discovering the higher races when we decided to pre-empt them by carrying out a ritual to send them a message. It basically amounted to, "We mean you no harm, but please keep our secret." Even after three weeks, they were taking their time catching on.

I barely tasted the questionable food as I chewed and swallowed, hyperaware of the man as he stood up and moved to sit across from me. The quality of his aura had changed from a dim blue signifying weariness to a crackling violet warning of confrontation, yet softened by pink curiosity. My belly clenched and I found it hard to swallow.

"You're like me, aren't you?" he said in a low voice. "Or . . . are you one of them?"

My pulse raced as I set down my sandwich and lifted my gaze to meet his. Dark brows curved over his gray-green eyes and his skin was a tawny brown about a shade lighter than my own. His thick black hair fell almost to his shoulders, mussed like he worried his hands through it often. He raked fingers through it, confirming my observation. The Adam's apple in his throat bobbed as he swallowed, and a piece of stone carved in the shape of a musical clef jiggled on its thong.

"What do you think?" I asked. "Am I like you, or like them?"

It wasn't really a test. I genuinely wanted to know. I was technically human—both my biological parents were human, at any rate—but I'd been ripped from my mother's womb shortly after conception, then grown in a tank and sustained with ancient nymphaea blood for the first five months of my existence.

Being so acutely conscious of every moment of my life,

even from those first glimmers of awareness after conception, should have made it easier for me to understand my
own nature . . . to know where I fit in. But it had only made it
infinitely harder.

I wasn't just human—the blood of the higher races that
ran in my veins defined me as much as my humanity did—
and part of the reason I'd run to begin with was to try to
understand what I was. I couldn't be everything; that was too
damn confusing. But at the moment, I didn't really feel like I
belonged anywhere at all. Maybe his observation would help
me understand.

He studied me for a moment longer, then shook his head
and frowned. "I think you're something else. But if you aren't
human, you have to be one of them, right? You just look so
normal. I mean . . . you're fucking gorgeous. They're all beautiful, but, um, you look mostly human."

I gave him a gentle smile and nodded, barely containing
my elation at having this conversation at long last, and with a
man as lovely to look at as he was. "I am mostly human. But
out of curiosity, what do you see that suggests otherwise?"

His half-eaten sandwich lay forgotten on his tray, though
he stared at it blindly for a second before looking at me
again. The divine glow that tinged his aura flared, reminding
me that though the bloodline was also *mostly* human, they
carried faint genetic mutations that linked them to the
higher races. More importantly, they were all carrying blood
that linked them to a god. That divine link had been dormant
until three weeks ago, the god at the other end of it on the
mend after a particularly brutal attack. But he was at full
power now, and so the bloodline was now at full awareness
of the higher races.

My new friend seemed to struggle for words, and my
heart went out to him. None of this could have been easy—
first to discover out of the blue that humanity wasn't the

only race with advanced intellect on the planet, and then that whatever traits marked him and the rest of the bloodline as special also made them targets for some invisible threat. But I had to know what it was he saw that identified the higher races.

Over the past three weeks since I'd left home, I'd learned to be cautious when I interacted with the bloodline. We may have been a little heavy-handed with the cautionary aspect of the spell we cast on them to protect our secrets. They avoided talking to *anyone* about us as a result, even each other, and were downright terrified of any of the higher races they came into contact with. Somehow I managed to fly under the radar. The higher races barely paid any attention to me when I came across them, and the bloodline just gave me odd looks, as if they wanted to say hello but were afraid of looking dumb.

This man was clearly willing to risk looking like an idiot to get it out, and I'd be damned if I was going to discourage him from talking.

"It's all right," I finally said, reaching across the table and squeezing his hand. His head jerked up as though I'd just shocked him and he stared at me. His hand tightened into a fist beneath my fingers and the intricate design on his forearm flexed. What looked like scales inked into his arm faded from deep red to bright turquoise.

"Fuck, you *are* one of them," he breathed. He relaxed his hand and spread his fingers out, then turned it over beneath mine until our palms touched. I got a view of the rest of his tattoo of a huge fish swimming amid stylized blue-green waves. Warmth radiated from his skin along with a spark of something more that made my breath catch.

The increased intimacy made me want to pull away, but he seemed on the verge of a revelation, so I left my hand in his grasp. Taking a deep breath, he said, "It's like you all resonate at a different frequency than the rest of us. Like the sunlight bounces off your skin differently, and sound waves travel around your bodies differently. But until a few weeks ago, I just didn't have the senses that could see and hear you properly."

Glancing up at the abrasive fluorescent lights, he chuckled. "Guess nobody's immune to crap lighting though, huh? It took me a few minutes to be able to tell after you sat down, but now . . ."

He slid his palm along mine. An electric charge passed through my hand into his skin. I pulled my hand back and rested it under the table on my lap, uncomfortable with the rising need that simple touch had elicited. I didn't need my dragon or my nymphaea nature waking up with this enticing stranger. Or at all, for that matter. There was too much at stake.

"What's your name?" he blurted, his eyes now bright with curiosity, the floodgates having opened up after our touch. "What kind are you? The message said there were four . . . ah . . . races? Are you a dra—"

He clamped his mouth shut and glanced around. The parking lot beyond the windows was nearly empty and the cafeteria was dead, aside from one lonely cashier reading a book near the self-serve stations across the room. At this time of night, the place was a graveyard.

"No, I'm not a dragon," I said. "Not exactly. My name's Deva Rainsong. I'm sort of an ambassador from all four races."

That sounded plausible; he didn't need to know that *what* I was, while it had a name, wasn't exactly definable. I was a chimera, a hybrid of not only the four higher races, but human too. And I was the only one of my kind.

He also didn't need to know that I had effectively run

away from home and was absolutely lost when it came to understanding my own nature.

"Day-va," he said, smiling as he drew out my name. "I'm Bodhi."

"I'm happy to meet you, Bodhi," I said, smiling slightly, but too apprehensive to make it stick. Thanks to his rippling aura and a particular quality to his words, I could sense he was about to ask me something and I wasn't going to have a good answer for him, which killed me.

"You guys have . . . abilities, right? Mystical powers?" He lowered his voice again as he shoved his tray aside and leaned closer to me. The desperation that had lain dormant during our interaction thus far flared to life, crackling though his aura.

I had to suppress a sigh because I knew what was coming.

"We do, to varying degrees," I said. I was using at least two of them already to interpret his true desires. Not only did my dragon nature give me the ability to read his aura for secrets about his state of mind, but I had the innate ability to hear the truth in people's spoken words—a trait I'd inherited from my turul side.

"My grandma's sick. The doctors don't have a clue what it is, but it started the same day the message came. It has to be linked. There must be something you can do."

"I can try," I said with a nod.

Swallowing a knot of helplessness, I stood. While I did have some abilities, those I was born with were woefully inadequate to do fuck-all for his grandmother. I hadn't spent the last three weeks in hospitals for my health, after all, or for the health of the victims I'd observed. Bodhi's grandma was not the first to fall prey to some mysterious creature that only seemed interested in members of the bloodline, and chances were that Bodhi himself would eventually become a target. And there wasn't a damn thing I could do about it.

But I could sure as hell try, and him inviting me to actually see his grandmother was the first break I'd had since this all began.

He grabbed both our trays and dumped the remnants of our midnight lunches in the trash, stacked the trays on top, then held the door open for me to follow.

"It's this way," he said, leading the way across a courtyard through another set of doors with an elevator on the other side. I could've found the way in my sleep.

When his grandmother had arrived, I was already here, having just watched a man fall into a coma as his soul fell to the beasts that had come for the bloodline. Before him, all the victims had died before I could see what had happened to them, but over the last few weeks they seemed to last longer, though I was beginning to lose hope that I'd be able to figure out how to actually heal them.

The two most recent victims were afflicted by a weakening of spirit that drained their will until they were nothing but feeble husks. The doctors had conducted every test imaginable, but they couldn't see what I could.

I braced myself when we exited the elevator by the fifth-floor nurses' station. The beasts were there, lurking in the shadows.

I glared at the creatures I'd taken to calling "soul hounds" as we passed through the door into Bodhi's grandmother's room. They were pair of shimmering, violet mirages that vanished when I looked directly at them, and inexplicably perked up whenever I arrived. One had a silver blaze down its face and the other had glowing, booted paws.

Both shadowy heads followed my passage. It was as if they were just biding their time until the woman died, but I'd be damned if I was going to let that happen.

The hounds spent their evenings pacing between the two victims, their foxlike ruffs shimmering with pale cascades of power from the energy they drained. Everything I'd tried to get them to leave only seemed to encourage them.

At least it wasn't a constant thing. They'd arrive in the dead of night when the hospital was quietest, their dim glows gradually brightening as they absorbed power from the souls of the afflicted, and they'd leave at daybreak. I had no idea where they went. They seemed completely disinterested in the normal humans who staffed the hospital; the only people they cared about were the pair whose life forces reached out with a shimmering magical tether to each of the hounds.

What would happen if and when one of the victims died, I had no idea—I'd only felt the prior deaths, not witnessed them—but I suspected they would move onto someone else in the bloodline, judging from how they sniffed around the family members who came and went, including Bodhi and a woman who I believed was his mother.

Bodhi's grandmother would be the first I'd actually see in person. I'd tried and failed on several occasions to talk my way in before.

The night nurse eyeballed me as I strolled by, and I gave her an exaggeratedly sweet smile when Bodhi opened his grandmother's door and motioned for me to enter. Hopefully I could learn something new from actually examining one of the victims.


*WANT TO READ THE REST?* **Buy now.**

# ABOUT OPHELIA BELL

Ophelia Bell loves a good bad-boy and especially strong women in her stories. Women who aren't apologetic about enjoying sex and bad boys who don't mind being with a woman who's in charge, at least on the surface, because pretty much anything goes in the bedroom.

Ophelia grew up on a rural farm in North Carolina and now lives in Los Angeles with her own tattooed bad-boy husband and six attention-whoring cats.

Subscribe to Ophelia's newsletter to get updates directly in your inbox. If newsletters aren't your thing, you can find her on social media.

http://opheliabell.com/subscribe

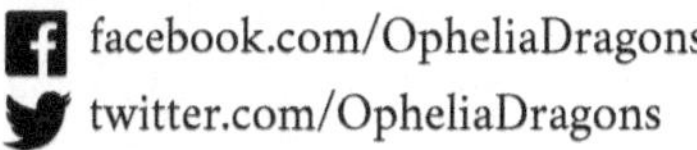

facebook.com/OpheliaDragons
twitter.com/OpheliaDragons

**Sleeping Dragons Series**

Animus

Tabula Rasa

Gemini

Shadows

Nexus

Ascend

Sleeping Dragons Omnibus

**Rising Dragons Series**

Night Fire

Breath of Destiny

Breath of Memory

Breath of Innocence

Breath of Desire

Breath of Love

Breath of Flame and Shadow

Breath of Fate

Sisters of Flame

Rising Dragons Omnibus

Dragon's Melody (a standalone dragon novel)

**Immortal Dragons Series**

Dragon Betrayed

Dragon Blues

Dragon Void

Dragon Splendor

Dragon Rebel

Dragon Guardian

Dragon Blessed

Dragon Equinox

Dragon Avenged

*Immortal Dragons Box Sets:*

Immortal Dragons: Books 1, 2, & 3 + Prequel

Immortal Dragons: Books 4-6 + Epilogue

**Black Mountain Bears**

Clawed

Bitten

Nailed

Stonetree Trilogy

**Fate's Fools Series**

Fate's Fools

Fool's Folly

Fool's Paradise

Fool's Errand

Nobody's Fool

Eye of the Hurricane

Fool's Bargain

April's Fools

Thieves of Fate

**Aurora Champions Series**

*(Set in Milly Taiden's "Paranormal Dating Agency" world)*

The Way to a Bear's Heart

Hot Wings

Triple Talons

Midnight Star

Once in a Dragon Moon

**Second Skin Series (Romantic Suspense)**

Mad Dog

Mile High

Valentine's Day

The Devil's Daughter

Marked Man

**Rebel Lust Taboo**

Casey's Secrets

Blackmailing Benjamin

Burying His Desires

Doubling Down

**Standalone Erotic Tales**

After You

Out of the Cold